The White Man's Foot by Grant Allen

Charles Grant Blairfindie Allen was born on February 24th, 1848 at Alwington, near Kingston, Canada West (now part of Ontario).

Home schooled until 13 when his family moved to England, Grant was to become a highly regarded science writer who branched out to a fiction career and became enormously popular.

His work helped propel several genres of fiction and whilst his career was short it was enormously productive.

Grant's scientific background enabled him to root much of his work in a plausibility that was denied to others. He had little fear in challenging a society that treated women as second class citizens and creating best sellers from such works.

On October 25th 1899 Grant Allen died at his home in Hindhead, Haslemere, Surrey, England. He died just before finishing Hilda Wade. The novel's final episode, which he dictated to his friend, doctor and neighbour Sir Arthur Conan Doyle from his bed appeared under the appropriate title, The Episode of the Dead Man Who Spoke in 1900.

Index of Contents

DEDICATION

TO JERRARD GRANT ALLEN,

THE ONLY BEGETTER OF THESE ENSUING ADVENTURES.

My Dear Grantie,

From the following pages, written with a single eye to your own personal tastes and predilections, you may, I trust, learn three Great Moral Lessons.

First, never to approach too near the edge of an active volcano.

Second, never to continue your intimacy with a man who deliberately and wickedly declines to pull you out of a burning crater.

And third, never to intrust the care of youth to a cannibal heathen South Sea Islander.

With the trifling exception of these three now enumerated, I am not aware that you can extract any Great Moral Lesson whatsoever from the hairbreadth escapes of Kea and her associates.

Having thus almost entirely satisfied your expressed wishes in this matter—for "a story without a moral"—I subscribe myself, with pride,

Your obedient servant and very loving father,

G.A.

CHAPTER I

My brother Frank is a most practical boy. I may be prejudiced, but it seems to me somehow there's nothing like close personal contact with active volcanoes to teach a young fellow prudence, coolness, and adaptability to circumstances. "Tom," said he to me, as we stood and watched the queer party on deck, devouring taro-paste as a Neapolitan swallows down long strings of macaroni: "don't you think, if we've got to live so long in a native hut, and feed on this port of thing, we may as well use ourselves to their manners and customs, whatever they may be, at the pearliest convenient opportunity?"

"Haven't you heard, my dear boy," said I, "what the naval officer wrote when he was asked to report to the Admiralty on that very subject of the manners and customs of the South Sea Islanders? 'Manners they have none,' he replied with Spartan brevity, 'and their customs are beastly.'"

"Not a bit of it," Frank answered quickly in his jolly way. "For my part I think this sticky, pasty stuff they're eating with their fingers, though it's a bit stodgy, looks like real jam, and I'd much rather take my lunch off things like that up here on deck, out of a native calabash, than go down and eat a civilized meal with a knife and fork in that hoky-poky, stuffy little cabin there."

I confess, for myself, I didn't exactly like the look of it. Cosmopolitan as I am, I object to fingers as a substitute for spoons. We were on board the Royal Hawaiian mail steamer Liké Liké, 500 tons registered burden, from Honolulu for Hilo, in the island of Hawaii; and a quainter group than the natives on deck I'm bound to admit, in all my wanderings, by sea or by land, I had never set eyes on. The tiny steamer was built in fact on purpose to accommodate all tastes alike, be the same savage or civilized. Down stairs was a saloon where regular meals in the European fashion were well served by a dusky Polynesian steward in a white linen jacket, to such luxurious persons as preferred to take them in that orthodox manner. But the unsophisticated natives, in their picturesque dress, believing firmly in the truth of the proverb that fingers were made before forks, liked better to carry their own simple provisions in their baskets with them. They picnicked on deck in merry little circles, laughing and talking at the top of their voices (when they weren't sea-sick) as they squatted on their mats of woven grass round the family taro-bowl. From this common dish, parents and children, young men and maidens, fed all alike, each dipping his forefinger dexterously into the sticky mess, and then twisting it round, as one might twist a lot of half-boiled toffee, till they landed it safely with a sudden twirl in their appreciative mouths. "It must be awfully good," Frank went on meditatively, eyeing the doubtful mixture with a hungry look. "They seem to enjoy it so, or else of course they wouldn't lick their fingers! I wish we could strike up a friendship now with some of these amiable light-coloured natives, and get them to share their lunch with us off-hand. I wonder what they call this precious stuff of theirs?"

"We call it taro," one of the nearest group answered, greatly to our surprise, in perfectly good and clear English. "Would you like to taste some? It's very nice. We shall be delighted if you'll try it. Hawaiians are always proud indeed to show any hospitality in their power to friendly strangers."

She was a pretty young girl of eighteen who spoke, lighter a good deal in complexion than most of the other natives around, and she was seated with a tall, dark, serious-looking old Hawaiian at a calabashful of the strange pasty mixture the appearance of which had so attracted Frank's favourable attention. As she spoke, she moved a little aside to make room for us on her mat, as if they were all playing Hunt-the-Slipper; and Frank, whose fault, I'm bound to admit, was never shyness, squatted down at once, nothing loth, tailor-fashion, on the deck by her side, and with many thanks accepted the courteous offer of a dip in the taro-bowl.

"Upon my word, Tom," he said, twirling a great dab of the queer-looking paste awkwardly into his mouth, "it's first-rate grub when you come to taste it. A little sour to be sure, but as good as pancakes. If you're going to feed us like this on the islands, sir," he added, turning to the stern old man, "I don't think we'll be in any hurry to run away again."

"Bring out some more food, Kea," the dark old Hawaiian half whispered to the girl politely, in English not quite so good as her own, but still very fluent, "and ask the gentleman," with a slight bow towards me, "if he won't be good enough to join us in our simple luncheon."

"I shall be only too glad," I answered, immensely surprised, and with some qualms of conscience about my unfortunate remark as to the manners and customs, which I never expected any native on board to understand. "It will be much more pleasant, I'm sure, to take my meals up here on deck than to go down to that hot and stuffy little saloon below."

As I seated myself, the girl Kea took up from her side a pretty basket of plaited palm-leaves, and produced from it a few pieces of dried fish, some cold roast pork, a stick or two of sugar-cane, several fresh oranges just picked from the tree, and a tempting display of bananas and bread-fruits. Frank and I were old enough sailors and old enough travellers to fare sumptuously off such excellent food stuffs; indeed we had just arrived in the Islands from San Francisco by the last mail steamer, and fresh fruit was a great luxury to us; while after so long a voyage on the open Pacific we thought nothing of this pleasant little summer cruise between the beautiful members of that volcanic archipelago.

A meal together is a capital introduction. In the course of ten minutes we were all four of us on excellent terms with one another. Kea had introduced to us the dark old man as her Uncle Kalaua, a Hawaiian chief of the old stock of some distinction, whose house was remarkable for being situated higher up the slopes of the great volcano, Mauna Loa, than any other on the entire island. She herself, she let us know by casual side-glimpses, was a half-caste by birth, though she hardly looked as dark as many Europeans; her mother had been Kalaua's only sister, and her father the captain of an English whaling-ship; but both were dead, she added with a sigh, and she lived now with her grim old uncle near the very summit of the great burning mountain. She told us a vast deal about herself, in fact, by way of introduction, with the usual frankness of the simple, unsophisticated children of nature, and she asked us a lot of questions in return, being anxious to learn, as we were neither missionaries, nor whalers, nor sugar-planters, nor merchants, what on earth our business could be in Hawaii.

"Well," said I, with a smile of amusement, "you'll think it a very funny one indeed when I tell you what it is. We've come to make observations on Mauna Loa."

"To make observations!" Kea answered with a faint thrill of solemn awe in her hushed voice. "Oh, don't say that. It's—it's so very dangerous." And she glanced aside timidly at her uncle.

Kalaua looked up at us quickly with a suspicious glance. "Observations on Mauna Loa?" he cried in a very stern tone. "On our great volcano? Scientific observations? The man is ill advised in truth who tries to go poking and prying too much about Mauna Loa!"

"Oh, you needn't be afraid," Frank answered laughing; "need they, Tom? It's not by any means our first experience of eruptions. My brother's an awful dab at volcanoes, you know. He's seen dozens; and he's been sent out to examine this one in particular by the British Association for the Advancement of Science. I'm his assistant-examiner, without salary. Sounds awfully grand that, doesn't it? But we mean to have a jolly lark in Hawaii for all that. Expenses paid, and all found; and nothing to do but to go down the crater and look about us. We expect to have a splendid time. There's nothing I love like a really good volcano."

But in spite of Frank's enthusiastic way of looking at the matter I could see at a glance that the mention of our object in visiting Hawaii had cast a shade of gloom at once over both Kea and her uncle. The old man seemed to grow moody and sullen; Kea was rather grieved and saddened. The rest of our meal passed off less pleasantly. It was not till we began to chew green sugar-cane together by way of dessert, that Kea's spirits at all returned. She laughed and talked then once more with native good-humour, showing us how to strip and peel the fresh cane, and making fun of us merrily because in our English awkwardness we got pieces of the fibre wedged hopelessly in between our front teeth. Yet even so I couldn't help suspecting that something was weighing upon her mind a little. Evidently they were either hurt or distressed that we should think of scientifically observing Mauna Loa. I wondered much whether they held the mountain too sacred a thing for inquisitive science to poke its nose into, or whether they only considered it too dangerous a crater for the bold explorer to meddle with carelessly. If it was merely the last, I didn't much mind. Frank and I were thoroughly at home with nasty-tempered volcanoes, and knew their tricks and their manners down to the ground far too well to be in the least afraid of them. I had been engaged in studying their manifestations indeed for the last six years; and Frank, who was born to face danger, had joined me in all my expeditions and explorations ever since he'd been big enough to carry a knapsack.

In the course of the afternoon however I happened to be standing with pretty little Kea near the bow of the steamer, while her uncle was slowly pacing the quarterdeck, immersed in conversation with a Hawaiian acquaintance. She was a graceful young girl, with a wreath of yellow flowers twined, Pacific fashion, round her broad straw hat, and another garland of crimson hibiscus thrown lightly like a scarf like one well-shaped shoulder. She glanced timidly round to see if Kalaua was well out of earshot; then, seeing herself safe, she said to me in a low, half-whispered voice, "If I were you, Mr. Hesselgrave, I'd give up the idea of exploring Mauna Loa."

"Give it up!" I cried. "Why, really, you know, that would be quite impossible! I've come all the way from England on purpose to visit it. Is the mountain so very dangerous then?"

Kea's voice dropped a tone lower still. "It's more than dangerous," she said very nervously. "It's almost certainly fatal."

"How so?" I asked. I was not easily frightened.

She hesitated a moment. Then she answered with a pained and half-terrified air, "Nobody in Hawaii will give you any assistance."

"Why not?" I inquired. "Are they all so dreadfully afraid of the volcano?"

"Not of the volcano," Kea replied with evident awe in her tone, "but of Pélé, of Pélé. I suppose you've never even heard about Pélé, though!"

"Never!" I repeated, laughing unconcernedly. "Enlighten my darkness. Who is he, or what is it?"

"It's neither he nor it," the Hawaiian girl answered in a hushed voice. "It's she, if it's anybody. Pélé's the goddess who lives, as our people used once to believe, in a fiery cave at the bottom of Mauna Loa!"

"Nonsense!" I replied, amused at the girl's apparent superstition. "I thought you were all converted here long ago. You don't mean to say your people go on believing still in such childish nonsense as gods and goddesses?"

Kea's voice sank lower than ever, and she glanced around her with a frightened little gaze. "We don't worship them, you know," she answered apologetically, under her breath almost; "but we can't help believing there's somebody there, of course, some super-natural being, when we hear Pélé groaning and moaning and sobbing in the dead of night, or see her casting up huge red-hot stones and showers of lava, whenever she's angry." She paused a moment: then she added mysteriously in a solemn undertone. "There must be something in it. My father knew that. He was one of the bravest and most skilful whalers in the whole Pacific, and he always said there was something in it."

I hadn't the heart to answer her back. I didn't consider the captain of a whaling ship a conclusive authority on such a point of science; but I couldn't bear to interfere with the poor girl's touching belief in her dead father's supreme wisdom; so I abstained humanely from adverse criticism. "And your uncle?" I asked after a brief interval.

Kea seemed almost terrified at the question. "My uncle," she said, in a shuffling way, "knows one thing well—that, according to the firm tradition of our ancestors, if the White Man's Foot ever treads the inner floor of Pélé's home, the White Man himself must foil a victim that day to the anger of the goddess. It may be true, or it may be false: but at any rate, that was what our fathers told us."

I laughed again. She was so absurdly and profoundly in earnest about it all. "In that case." I said with a little bow, "I may as well make my will at once, and leave my property to my nearest relations, for it's all up with me. I mean to explore the crater myself, and, I need hardly tell you, Frank will accompany me. We'll call in some morning at the front door, and drop a card on this terrible Pélé. I hope the lady will have the politeness to be at home to receive visitors."

The girl shuddered. "Hush," she cried, with a terrified face. "Don't talk like that. Don't talk any more about the matter at all. You don't know what you're saying. My uncle is coming. I wouldn't for worlds he should overhear us. We don't believe in Pélé any longer, of course. But I hope for all that you'll never try to explore the crater."

At that very moment the old chief Kalaua, who had long been deeply immersed in talk with his friend at the stern, apparently discussing some serious subject, strolled up and joined us. He bowed once more as he approached, with the strange old savage Hawaiian politeness; for in courtesy of manner these Pacific Islanders could give points to most educated Englishmen. "I was thinking," he said, withdrawing his cigar and addressing me, "that if you and your brother really want to make explorations in Mauna Loa you couldn't do better than come up and stop at my house on the top of the mountain. It's nearest the summit of any in the island, and it would be a convenient place for you always to start from on your exploring expeditions. You'd save the long ride up the slopes. May I venture to offer you the hospitality of a humble Hawaiian roof? It's a nice warm house, European built, it was put up by my English brother-in-law, Kea's father; and I think we could manage to make you as comfortable as anybody in Hawaii. Is it agreed? What say you?"

"You would allow me to pay for our board and lodging, of course?" I answered interrogatively. "Otherwise I mustn't trespass so far as that on your kind indulgence."

The old native drew himself up at once with offended dignity. "I'm a chief," he replied with quiet emphasis. "The blood of the great Kamehameha the First flows in my veins. When I ask you to my house, I ask you as my guest. Don't offend me, I beg of you, by offering me money!"

I felt I had really hurt the old chief's pride and wounded his feelings, so I hastened to apologize with the best expressions I could summon up, and to protest that I hadn't the remotest intention of slighting in any way his generous offer. "In England," I continued, "we are not accustomed to be received by perfect strangers in such a princely style of open-handed hospitality."

Kalaua bowed. "It is well," he answered with stately dignity. "Come to my house, and you shall have all that my house affords freely. May we expect you to stop with us then? It will give myself and my niece the greatest pleasure in life, I assure you, to receive you."

Kea from behind framed her lips, to my surprise, into an emphatic "No." I saw it and smiled. She uttered no sound, but the old man seemed instinctively to recognize the fact that she was making signs to me. He turned round, half-angrily, though with perfect composure, and said something to her in Hawaiian, which I did not then fully understand, though I had been studying the language hard, with dictionary and grammar, all the way out on my voyage from England. Kea looked frightened and held her tongue at once. The old chief glanced back at me for a decisive answer. In spite of Kea's warning I thought the opportunity too good to be missed. "I shall be delighted," I answered with my warmest manner. "I'm sure it's most kind of you. How can I thank you enough? I had no idea you Hawaiians were so generously hospitable."

When I told Frank of it that young rascal remarked with a solemn grin, "Of course they're hospitable! Why, didn't they take in Captain Cook, and roast him and eat him, they were so very fond of him? I expect that's what this sober old fellow of yours means to do with us. He'll give a dinner-party in our honour when we get there, no doubt, and you and I will be the joints for the occasion. That's the Pacific way of welcoming a stranger."

CHAPTER II

"When we reached Hilo, I went ashore in a boat through the dangerous surf, and before arranging to go up the mountain with my host and his niece, I called first on an English merchant in the little palm-girt town, to whom we had letters of introduction from friends in Liverpool.

"Going to stop with Kalaua, eh?" the merchant said, as soon as we had named our particular business. "A very good house, too! You couldn't do better. Quite close to the very mouth of the crater, and right in the track of the great red-hot lava streams. You'll see Pélé kicking up a shindy there simply to perfection. Her majesty's been getting precious uneasy of late, rumbling and growling I shouldn't be surprised if you're just in the nick of time for a first-rate eruption."

"And what sort of person is my host?" I asked curiously. "He seems a very stern, old-fashioned cannibal."

Our new acquaintance laughed. "You may well say that," he answered smiling. "In the good old days, or the bad old days, whichever of the two you prefer to call them, you pays your money and you takes your choice, Kalaua, they say, was the hereditary priest of that grim goddess, Pélé. His house was built on the highest habitable point of the mountain where Pélé dwells, that he might be close at hand to appease the angry spirit of the great crater whenever she began to pour down lava over the banana-grounds and cocoanut plantations at the foot of the volcano. Many a fat pig, and many a basketful of prime taro that hard-looking old man has offered up in his time to Pélé, ay, and I dare say many a human victim, too, if we only knew it. But all that's over long ago, thank goodness. He's a Christian now, of course, like all the rest of them; a very respectable old fellow in his way, with a keen eye of his own to business, and a thorough comprehension of the state of the sugar market. He keeps a good house. You've fallen on your feet, I can tell you, for Hawaii, if you've got an invitation to stop for an indefinite time as a guest at Kalaua's."

I was glad to hear we had happened by chance upon such comfortable quarters.

We slept that night at a little Hawaiian inn at Hilo, where we dined most sumptuously off roast pig and baked plantains; and at six next morning, Kalaua himself wakened us up to start on our long ride up the great lone mountain.

When we sallied forth, four sure-footed ponies stood saddled at the door, and Kalaua, Kea, Frank, and myself, mounting our careering steeds (only they didn't career), began our ascent to the cloud-capped summit. Mauna Loa, that bald cone, is almost as high as any peak in the Alps, rising some 14,000 feet above sea level; but the ascent over the lava plains is gentle and gradual, and the top, in this warm and delicious climate, still remains far below the level of perpetual snow. Nevertheless it is a long and tedious ride, some thirty miles, from Hilo to the top; and our sure-footed little ponies clambered slowly on, planting their hoofs with the utmost deliberation on the treacherous surface of the rugged and honey-combed masses of lava. Frank and I were both quite tired out with their camel-like pace when we reached the summit. Kea and Kalaua, more accustomed to the ascent, were as fresh as daisies, and Kea, in particular, laughed and talked incessantly, though I fancied, she was ill at ease somehow, in spite of all her apparent merriment.

At last, after crossing a wide expanse of broken blocks of black basalt, as big as the largest squares of freestone used in architecture, and then sliding and gliding over a hideous expanse of slippery, smooth lava, like ice for glassiness, we pulled up, wearied, at a house built close on the very summit, European or rather American, in its style and arrangements, but comfortable and even wealthy-looking in all its appointments. It was composed of solid volcanic stone, cut into large square masses, and round it ran a pleasant wooden verandah, with rocking-chairs temptingly displayed in a row under its broad canopy. An oleander blossomed profusely by the side, and tropical creepers of wonderful beauty festooned the posts and balconies with their hanging verdure and their trumpet-shaped flower-bells.

"Come in," Kea cried, leaping down with ease from her mountain pony, which a native boy seized at once and took away to the stables. "Come in, and make yourselves at home in our house. Dinner will be ready in twenty minutes."

"I should hope so," Frank answered, with his free-and-easy manner; "for I'm free to confess I want my grub awfully after such a long ride. And then I shall go out and inspect this precious volcano we hear so much about."

Kalaua's brow darkened somewhat, as if he didn't like to hear Mauna Loa so cavalierly described, and he murmured a few words in Hawaiian to Kea, in which I could only catch the name of Pélé, repeated very earnestly several times over.

The house was large, roomy, and well furnished, with bamboo chairs and neat native bedsteads; and the dinner, to which Frank at least did full justice, seemed to promise well for our future treatment under the old chief's hospitable roof. Kalaua himself grew somewhat less grim, too, as the meal progressed. Nothing thaws the soul like dinner. He warmed by degrees, and told us several amusing stories of the old heathen days, delighting Frank's heart by narrating, in glowing language, how, in his youth, he had charged, a naked warrior at the head of his naked troops, when Kamehameha the Second attacked the island. Frank was charmed to find himself so nearly face to face with aboriginal savagery. "And what did you do with the prisoners?" he asked inauspiciously.

The old man smiled a grimly terrible smile. "The less said about the prisoners the better," he answered at last, with some faint show of conventional reluctance. "Remember, we were heathens then, and knew no better. The English have come since and taught us our duty. We no longer fight; we are civilized now; we buy horses, and cultivate yam and bread-fruit and sugar-cane." And he helped himself as he spoke to another piece of fresh ginger.

I don't think Frank quite saw what he meant; but I confess a shudder passed through my own frame as I realized exactly what the old chief was driving at. It was strange to stand so very close to the lowest barbarism known to humanity. They had eaten the prisoners.

After dinner we strolled out, in the beautiful, clear, tropical evening, to the edge of the crater. Accustomed as I was to volcanoes everywhere, I never beheld a more grand or beautiful sight than that first glimpse of Mauna Loa in all its glory. We looked over the edge of the great ring of basalt, and saw below us, down three successive ledges of rock, seething and tossing, a vast and liquid sea of fire. Here and there the lava boiled and bubbled into huge, inflated, balloon-like crests; here and there it rose into monstrous black stacks and irregular chimneys, from whose fiery mouths belched forth great columns of red flame, interspersed with dark wreaths of smoke and sulphur. It was the wildest, noblest, and most awful volcano I had ever yet visited, and my acquaintance with the family was by no means superficial. Frank stood aghast with awe and wonder for a moment by my side. "Why, Vesuvius is nothing to it!" he cried, astonished, "and Etna's just nowhere in the matter of craters! I say, Tom, how I should love to see it in a good tip-top blazing eruption!"

As he spoke Kea, who had come out with us, clad from head to foot in her simple, long Hawaiian robe, gazed steadily over the brink, and looked down with a familiar glance into the gigantic crater. For a minute or two she kept her eyes fixed on a certain jagged peak or furnace of lava, round whose base the sea of liquid fire was surging and falling, like water in a saucepan on a kitchen stove. At last she broke out into sudden surprise, "Why, it's rising!" she cried breathlessly. "It's rising! It's rising!"

"How jolly!" Frank called out from a few yards down, where he had clambered to get a better view of the inner crater. "I hope that fellow in the town was right after all, and that we're going to come in at the very right point for a regular good eruptive outburst!"

Kea's face grew pale with terror. "You are," she answered, "I can see it rise. The bubbles are bursting; the steam's crackling. It always does so before it begins to flow out upon the slopes of the mountain."

She was quite right. It was clearly rising. I was overjoyed. Nothing could have happened more neatly or opportunely for the interests of science. Our arrival at Mauna Loa seemed to prove, as it were, the signal for the mountain to burst out at once into full activity. We were in luck's way. We had come on the very eve of an eruption.

Kea ran down to fetch her uncle. The old man came up, and peered over cautiously into the depths of the crater. Then he called aloud in Hawaiian to his trembling niece. I couldn't catch all the words he said, but I caught one sentence twice repeated, "Pélé ké loa," and a single word that recurred over and over again in his frantic outbursts, "Areoi," "Areoi."

I had brought my Hawaiian-English pocket dictionary with me from Hilo, and I turned up the words in their places one by one, to see if I could understand them. To my great surprise I found I had heard them quite aright; it's so hard to catch any part of an unknown language when rapidly spoken between natives. "Pélé ké loa," I discovered, meant in English, "Pélé is angry," and "areoi" was defined by my book as "a stranger, a foreigner, especially a white man, a European or American."

We stood long on the brink of the crater and watched it rising slowly before our very eyes. Kea pointed out to us with demonstrative finger the various floors or ledges on the inner wall. "That first," she said with an awestruck face, "is the Floor of the Strangers; as far as that everybody may go; it is as it were the mere threshold, or outer vestibule, of the volcano. The second, that you see further down below, in the dark glare, is the Floor of the Hawaiians; as far as that, by the rule of our fathers, only natives may dare to penetrate. If a white man's foot ever treads that floor, our people used to say, Pélé will surely claim him for her victim. The third, that you can just distinguish down there in the bright light, where the fiery lava is this moment rising, that's the Floor of Pélé: none but the priests of Pélé might venture in the old days to tread its precincts. If any other man or woman were to dream of descending upon it, in the twinkling of an eye, like a feather in the flame, our fathers said, Pélé would surely shrivel him to ashes."

"And you believe all that nonsense?" I cried incredulously.

Kea turned towards me with a very grave face. "It isn't nonsense," she answered, in her most serious manner. "It's perfectly true. As true as anything. Of course I don't believe the superstition, but whoever falls into that third abyss is burnt to a cinder before aid can arrive, by the wrath of the volcano."

"I dare say," I answered carelessly. "It looks quite hot enough to frizzle up anything. Whoever falls into an ordinary blast furnace (if it comes to that) is burnt to a cinder before aid can arrive, by the unconscious wrath of the molten metal."

"Don't talk so!" Kea cried, with a terrified face. "You distress me. You frighten me."

The volcano meanwhile rose faster and faster. The gray evening began to close in. A deep red glow spread over the open mouth of the crater. The clouds above reflected and repeated the lurid light. Every moment the glare grew deeper and yet deeper. As night came on, it seemed to rain fire. I saw at once that we were in for a good thing. We had hit on the exact moment of a first-class eruption.

A more awful or grander night than that I never remember. I'm a scientific man, and my business is to watch and report upon volcanoes; but that night, I confess, was every bit as hot as I care to have it. Anything hotter than that, indeed, would fry one like a herring. By nine o'clock, the mountain was in full glare; by ten, it was pouring out red fragments of stone and showers of ashes; by eleven, a stream of white glowing lava was pushing its way in one desolating flood down the ravines on the southern slope of the mountain. Before the final outburst, light curling wreaths of vapour ascended from fissures in the wall of the crater, and hung like a huge umbrella over the mountain top. The red glare, reflected from this strange cloud-like canopy, gave the whole scene for many miles around the appearance of being lighted up by giants at play with some vast and colossal Bengal fires. We looked on awestruck. Suddenly, and without the slightest warning, a sound reached our ears, a terrific sound, as of ten thousand engines blowing off steam; and all at once a great body of gas was ejected into the air, in a blaze of light, while huge fragments of rock were hurled violently upward, only to fall again in fiery heat upon the naked slopes of the cone and shoulders. All night long we were positively bombarded with these aërial shells; they fell in thousands round us on every side, though fortunately none of them happened to touch either the house itself or any one of its inhabitants.

Not a living soul remained upon the spot save Frank and myself, and Kea and her uncle. All the rest of the natives fled headlong down in wild panic and terror to the sea at Hilo.

A man of science, however, like a soldier on the battle-field, must know how to take his life in his hand. I got out my pencil, my sketch-book and my colours, and, true to the orders of the Association in whose interest I was travelling, I endeavoured to reproduce, as well as I could, in a spirited sketch, the whole awful scene as it unfolded itself in vivid hues before us. Frank, who is certainly the most intrepid boy of my acquaintance, ably seconded me in my difficult task. Kea looked on at us in speechless amazement. "Aren't you afraid?" she asked at last, in a hushed voice.

"Yes," I answered boldly, telling the plain truth, "if you will allow me to say so, I'm very much afraid indeed. But I'm a man of science; I've got to do it; and I shall do it still till the lava comes down and drives us away bodily. And you? Aren't you afraid, too, of the stones and ashes?"

"No," she replied, though her tone belied her. "The eruptions never hurt my uncle nor me. You see, he's been accustomed to them from his childhood upward. In the old days, he was taught to think he was under Pélé's protection."

Frank looked up, imperturbable as ever. "For my part," he said, tossing the curls from his forehead, "I'm not a man of science, like Tom, you know; and I'm not under the protection of a heathen goddess, like you and your uncle, Kea; but I call it the grandest set of fireworks I ever saw in all my life, beats the Crystal Palace hollow, and I wouldn't have missed it for fifty pounds, I can tell you."

As for Kalaua, he stood sombre, alone, with folded arms and tight-pressed lips, looking down unmoved into the depths of the crater.

CHAPTER III

All night long we remained outside on the platform of the summit, watching and sketching that terrific convulsion. The mountain poured forth endless floods of lava. Heaven and earth were lighted up with its awful glow. Kalaua stood by us still, erect and grim, like one conscious that the fiery hail and the red-hot boulders had no terrors for him, and could not harm him. Kea, pale and tremulous, yet too brave at heart to flinch ever so, crouched by his side, too awestruck to speak in mute expectation. Frank alone seemed undisturbed by the appalling commotion going on around him. Boy enough to feel nothing of the terror of the moment, he was simply excited by the grandeur and magnificence of that wonderful pyrotechnic display. "It's the jolliest sight I ever saw, Tom," he exclaimed with delight more than once during the evening. "Why, to live here would be almost as good as to have a season-ticket all the year round for all the fêtes and gala-days in England!"

By morning however the eruption slackened; the internal fires had worn themselves out. "Pélé has grown tired of kicking up such a rumpus," Frank remarked cheerfully; and as he himself was tired of watching her, too, he proposed we should go in and rest ourselves a little after our arduous labours. Indeed, the lava was now almost ceasing to flow, and the bombardment of pumice-stone and fiery cinders had intermitted a little. We returned to the house, and flung ourselves down on our beds in the clothes we wore, too fatigued after our long and sleepless watch to trouble ourselves with the needless bother of undressing. When you've sat up all night observing an eruption, you don't much care about such luxuries of an advanced civilization as nightshirts. Before we retired however Kea brought us in a big bowl of fresh taro-paste, and on this simple food we made a most excellent and substantial breakfast. In ten minutes we were snoring so hard on our bamboo beds that I don't believe even another eruption would have roused us up, if it had thundered at our doors with one of its monstrous subterranean boulders.

It was five in the evening before we woke again. Frank stretched himself with a yawn. "I don't know how you feel, Tom," he cried as he jumped out of bed, "but I feel as if that extinct instrument, the rack, had been invented over again for my special benefit. There's not a bone in my body that isn't aching."

"What does that matter," I answered, "if science is satisfied? I've got the very finest sketch of a first-class eruption that ever was taken since seismology became a separate study."

"Bother seismology!" Frank exclaimed with a snort. "What a jolly long word for such a simple thing! As if one couldn't say straight out, earthquakes. For my part, what I want satisfied isn't science at all, but an internal yearning for some breakfast or some supper, whichever you choose to call it."

The supper was soon upon the board (for by this time the native servants had returned), and as soon as it was finished, we sallied forth, all four together, to inspect the changes wrought in the mountain by last night's events. The effects of the eruption were indeed prodigious. Great streams of fresh lava still lay dull and half-hot along the fertile valleys of the mountain side; and the ground about the house was strewn thick and deep with a white coat of powdery ashes. "This is splendid!" I said. "I shall have my work cut out for me now for several weeks. Nobody had ever a better chance afforded him of observing in detail the effects of a great volcanic effort."

Kalaua glanced grimly across at me as I spoke. "I wonder," he murmured, with a sort of sphinx-like sardonic smile, "you have escaped so safe to observe and report upon them."

"Ah, you see, chief," Frank answered carelessly, "he was under your protection. Pélé wouldn't hurt us, you know, as we were guests of a friend of hers. That was awfully nice of her. She's a perfect lady, as volcanoes go. I call her a most polite and obliging goddess."

Kalaua turned away with a half angry look. It was clear that, converted or unconverted, he considered the terrible deity of his fathers no proper subject for light chaff or jesting.

We spent the next six weeks pleasantly enough in the old man's house, observing and making notes upon the curious facts connected with the crater and its recent outbreak. I will not narrate my results here at full for fear of boring you, the more so, as I have already devoted two large volumes to the subject in the British Association Reports, Manchester Meeting. It will be enough for the present to mention that Frank and I thoroughly explored the whole top of the crater, as far as the first floor, which Kea had described to us as the Floor of the Strangers. We measured and mapped it out in every direction with theodolite and chain, and we made numerous interesting, and, I venture to add, important observations upon the most disputed points in the phenomena of eruptions. We knew our way about the Floor of the Strangers, in fact, as well as we knew our way down from our own home at Hampstead Heath to Charing Cross Station. Kalaua and Kea were surprised to find how accurately we had learnt the whole geography of the district; and Kalaua in particular seemed far from pleased at our perfect familiarity with the mountain and its ways, though he was much too polite ever to say so openly, holding his peace on the matter, at least to our faces, with true antique Hawaiian courtesy. For bland courtesy of demeanour, commend me to a cannibal.

One morning however about six weeks after our first arrival, I had occasion to send Frank by himself down to Hilo, on one of the sure-footed little mountain ponies, to fetch up some ropes and other articles we needed for our exploration from the stores in the town; and I said good-bye to him just outside the house, where Kalaua was seated, smoking a cigarette, and wrapped up as usual in his own stern and sombre reveries.

"Good-bye, old fellow,"' Frank cried in farewell, as he mounted his horse and cantered gaily off. "Mind you take care of yourself while I'm away. Give the crater a wide berth. Don't try to go exploring any further without me!"

"All right," I shouted back. "I won't get into mischief. Trust me for saving my own skin. I shall just potter about a bit to amuse myself alone on the outer edge of the Floor of the Strangers."

"What do you want the rope for?" Kalaua asked moodily, looking up from his cigarette as Frank rode away. "Better not go trusting yourself with any rope too far in the crater of Mauna Loa."

"I'm not afraid," I answered, with a short little laugh. "I want the rope to let myself down to the lower levels."

"What, the Floor of the Hawaiians?" the old chief cried with flashing eyes.

"Well, yes," I answered; "that first, of course, and then, after that, the Floor of Pélé."

If I had dropped a bomb-shell right in front of his house, the stern old chief could not have looked that moment more appalled and horrified. "Young man," he cried, rising hastily to his feet and standing like a messenger of fate before me, "I warn you not to trifle with the burning mountain. Tread the Floor of the Strangers as much as you like, but the lower ledges of the crater are very dangerous. You're my guest, and I advise you. For unskilled feet to approach those levels is almost certain death. In the dark old days when we were all heathen, we used to say in our folly that the wrath of Pélé would burn you up like a leaf if you ventured to touch them. We no longer say that: we know better now. But we still say to all who would tamper with them that the mouth of the crater is most treacherous and perilous."

"Oh," I answered lightly, turning on my heel, "don't trouble for me. I'm accustomed to volcanoes. I don't object I think no more of them than a sailor thinks of chapters of a storm at sea. Let them boil and seethe as much as they like. They're nothing after all, when a fellow's used to them."

The old man answered me never a word. He rose, and with a gesture of solemn dissent wrapped his native cloak severely round him; then he walked in grim and gloomy silence back by himself into his own chamber.

As for me, I strolled off quietly, sketch-book in hand, up to the broken brink of the great crater. I had nothing in particular to do that morning, having in fact by this time quite exhausted the first ledge or Floor of the Strangers: and I could accomplish no work, now I had finished there, till Frank returned from town with the rope to lower us down to the Floor of the Hawaiians, the next ledge that I thought of mapping. So I sat myself down on a jagged peak of hardened cinders, cemented together by molten volcanic matter, and began in a lazy, idle, half-sleepy kind of way to sketch a distant point of the interior crater.

I had sat there listlessly, sketching and musing, for about twenty minutes, when I saw a sight I can never resist. A beautiful butterfly, of a species quite new to me, attracted my attention on the side of the crater-wall over which my legs were carelessly dangling. Now, though I am by trade (saving your presence) a seismologist and vulcanologist, no offence meant by those awesome words, I've always had a sneaking kindness in an underhand way for other departments of natural science, especially zoology; and a new butterfly, with a red spot on its tail, is a severe temptation that my utmost philosophy can never induce me to disregard under any circumstances. There are some scientific men, I know, who seem to think science ought to be made as dull and as dry and as fusty as possible: for my own part, I never could take that eminently correct and respectable view: I like my science as amusing as I can get it, with a considerable spice of adventure thrown in; and I prefer specimen-hunting among the Pacific Islands to name-hunting among the prodigiously learned and stupid memoirs of the British Museum. Between ourselves, too (but I wouldn't like this to reach the ears of the Royal Society), I regard a man as much more useful to science when engaged in catching birds or insects in the Malay Archipelago or the African mountains than when inventing names for them out of his own head in a fusty, dusty, musty room in the museum at South Kensington. Have the kindness to keep this dark however if you ever go to a British Association Meeting: for if it reached the ears of the Committee, they might think me an unfit person to entrust with any further volcanic investigations.

Well, my butterfly was resting, poised like a statue, on a pretty flowering plant that grew out of a cranny in the sheer wall of rock, a yard or two below the precise point where I was then sitting. Said I to myself, with an eager dart forward, "I shall nab that specimen;" and laying aside my pencil and drawing-pad at once, I proceeded forthwith, at the top of my speed, incontinently to nab him.

It was with great difficulty however that I clambered down the side of the crag, for the lava just there was porous and bubbly. It crumbled and broke like thin ice under my feet; and wherever I thought I had just secured myself a firm foothold it gave way after a moment, bit by bit, with the force of my pressure. Nevertheless I managed somehow, to my great delight, to reach the plant that sprouted from the cranny without at all disturbing my friend the butterfly, who, engrossed on his dinner, was hardly expecting an attack from the rear; and clapping my hand upon him before he could say Jack Robinson, I popped him, triumphant, into my pocket collecting case. Then, with a light heart, and the proud consciousness of a duty performed, I turned once more to climb up the cliff again.

But that, I found, was by no means so easy a matter as descending. I had got down partly by the mean and illegitimate device of letting my feet slide; to get back I must somehow secure a firm and certain foothold in the loose lava. To my surprise and horror there was none to be found. The soft and creamy pumice-stone seemed nowhere to afford a single solid point of support. I struggled in vain to recover my balance; at last, to my dismay, I stumbled and fell—fell, as I feared, towards the Floor of the Hawaiians, that yawned a full hundred and twenty feet of sheer depth in the crater below me. With a wild lunge I clutched for support at the plant in the cranny. It broke short in my hand, and my one chance gone, I rolled down rapidly to the very bottom. I didn't exactly tumble down the entire sheer height in a single fall; if I had I shouldn't be here to tell you. I broke the force of the descent somewhat by digging my hands and feet with frantic efforts into the loose wall of rotten lava. But before I could realize precisely what was happening I lost my head. The world reeled round me; my eyes closed. Next moment I was aware of a horrid thud, and a fierce blow against some hard surface. I knew then just where I had landed. I had fallen or rolled by stages the whole way down the crag, and was lying on my side on the Floor of the Hawaiians!

CHAPTER IV

My first thought, as I lay half-stunned and almost unconscious upon that naked bed of hard black rock, was that at any rate I had caught and fairly boxed my butterfly. My second, a much less agreeable one to encounter, was that I had certainly broken my leg in my full to the bottom.

I was conscious, in fact, of a dull but very deep-seated pain in my right thigh. I tried to move it. The agony was intense. It threw me back into my momentary faint again. For a minute or two I could hardly realize my position. Then it slowly came home to me by gradual stages that I was lying helpless, with a broken leg, unseen and unattended, on the Floor of the Hawaiians, a hundred and twenty feet down the gap of the crater.

Would anybody come to help me? I wondered. That was more than doubtful. As a rule, the whole day passed on those lonely heights without anybody approaching the mouth of the volcano, let alone climbing down by the zig-zag path into the floor above me. Kalaua's household were the sole frequenters of that solitary spot. However, Frank would at least be back from Hilo by six o'clock, or thereabouts, and then he would be sure to come up and look for me, when he missed me from my accustomed place on the verandah. I took out my watch, in order to see how long I might have to lie there in frightful pain, waiting for my brother's return to save me. We had learnt early rising with a vengeance since we came to the islands, breakfast at Kalaua's was at six sharp, to my horror, I found it was even now only half-past seven!

More than ten weary, dreary hours to watch and wait, with my broken leg, in that dismal crater!

It was an unpleasant outlook. I gazed around and tried to take in the situation.

Above me, a steep black wall of granite rose sheer and straight towards the open heaven. Below me, I could hear, though I could not see, the lake of liquid fire hissing and bubbling with horrible noises in its eternal cauldron. Around, the floor was composed of solid dark green obsidian, as hard and transparent and sharp as bottle-glass. I must lie as best I could, on my uneasy bed, and brave it out for ten hours somehow.

Fortunately, I soon discovered that as long as I lay quite still, the pain of my leg was comparatively trifling. It was only when I moved or stirred restlessly that it hurt me much, and then, the agony was enough to drive one frantic. I laid down my watch, to mark the time, on the rock in front of me. Happily, being a good naval chronometer, it had not been injured in the shock of my fall. I had nothing to do now but to count the hours till Frank could come up and relieve me at last from my awkward and even dangerous situation.

Ten hours is a very long time, with a broken leg, in the crater of Mauna Loa.

The floor of the ledge, I observed, as I gazed around, was covered with long strings of dark thread-like lava, as thin and delicate as a spun-glass tissue. These strings are a well-known product of the volcanic action of Mauna Loa, and the natives call them "Pélé's hair." They look upon them as the veritable tresses of the goddess. Having nothing else to do, I picked some up and examined it closely. No wonder the superstitious old Hawaiians took it in their time for the actual combings of their dread goddess's hair! I never in my life saw anything so exactly resembling human locks, at a first rough glance: and I was not surprised that even Kea herself should regard it as a token of the presence of that mysterious being who dwelt, as she still half believed, all alone among the eternal fires of the great crater.

Eight o'clock, nine o'clock, ten o'clock, passed, and I began by that time to get most unfeignedly weary of my enforced imprisonment. It was impossible to lie in one position all the time; and whenever I turned, or even moved, my leg gave me the most excruciating jerks of pain and agony. I was heartily sick now of the crater and all that belonged to it. What on earth, I thought, made me ever take to such a trade as vulcanology? I said to myself more than once in my despair that henceforth I'd give up volcanoes forever, and go in for some safe and honest trade, like a light-house-man's or an inspector of mines, for a livelihood.

About half-past ten however, as I lay half dozing with fatigue and pain, an incident occurred which broke the monotony of the situation: my attention was suddenly and vividly aroused by a noise that sounded like the report of a pistol.

What on earth could it be? I raised myself on my arms and gazed all round. The crater of Mauna Loa was a queer place indeed for even the most enthusiastic sportsman to come shooting in. The only game he could expect to find in such a spot would be surely salamanders. But firing was without doubt going on in the crater, not indeed on the floor on which I myself lay, but strange to say, on the other and still deeper ledges below me. As I strained my ear to listen, I heard frequent reports of pistols, one after another, in all directions down the hollow of the crater.

Then, with a sudden flash of recollection it burst in upon my memory that Frank and I had heard similar reports the year before on the slopes of Hecla, just on the eve of a serious eruption, when we were engaged in investigating the volcanoes of Iceland.

In a second, the appalling and terrible truth came home to me in all its ghastly awfulness. The lava in the crater must be rising explosively!

I was never much frightened of a volcano before, but that moment, I confess, I felt distinctly nervous.

From where I lay, I couldn't see over into the lake of liquid fire below, and my broken leg made it almost impossible for me to move or even to drag myself towards the steep edge, where I could gaze down into the abyss and make sure whether the lava was really rising. But such suspense was more than one could bear. With a supreme effort I raised myself a second time, very cautiously, upon my two hands and my left knee, and, trailing my right leg with difficulty behind me, I crawled or crept with unspeakable pain over yards of rough rock to the brink of the precipice.

An ineffable sight there met my eye. The black slaggy bottom of the huge crater, which generally reposed in tranquil peace like a calm sea, just broken here and there by fiery fissures, was now transformed into one bubbling mass of flame and vapour, all alive with a horrible livid glare, that lit up its seething and blazing billows with an awful distinctness. Loud, snorting puffs of steam burst thick and fast from the gaping fissures, and from many of the chinks great jets of molten material were willing out in huge floods, and rising gradually towards the Floor of Pélé, the third and last ledge immediately below me. If the eruption continued for two hours longer at its present rate, by half-past twelve, I felt fully convinced, the sea of lava would be wildly surging and roaring above the very spot whence I now surveyed it.

What was to be done? I lay and pondered.

Unless somebody came to my rescue meanwhile, I had only two hours more to live on earth; and then inch by inch I would be scorched to death, in unspeakable agony, before an advancing tide of liquid fire, by the most awful fate ever known to humanity!

It was ghastly; it was horrible: but I had to face it.

I peered over the edge, and watched with eager and tremulous awe the gradual approach of the devouring fire-flood. Slowly, slowly, foot by foot, and yard by yard, my inanimate enemy rose and rose, and rose again, by constant, cruel, crawling stages. Not always regularly, but in fluctuating billows. At times the molten sea leapt upward with a bound; at times it fell again, in a vast sink-hole, like some huge collapsing bubble of metal; but all the while, in spite of every apparent fluctuation, it mounted steadily in the long run up the black wall of rock, as the tide rises over a shelving beach, with its hideous gas jets hissing and groaning, and its angry flames drawing nearer and nearer each moment to devour me.

I lay there horror-stricken, and gazed idly down.

Nothing on earth that I myself could do would now avail me in any way to escape my destiny. I tried to turn and attempt the wall behind me. I might as well have tried to scale the naked side of a smooth and polished granite monument. The crag was like glass. There was nothing for it but to lie back in quiet and await my death as a brave man should await it. Science had had many martyrs before. I felt sure, as I lay there, that I too was to be numbered upon the increasing roll-call of its illustrious victims.

It is easy enough to fight and die; but to lie still and be slowly roasted to death, that, I take it, is quite a different matter.

Eleven o'clock went past on my watch. Ten, twenty, thirty, forty minutes. The fire had mounted half way up the side of the ledge on which I lay. I could feel its hot breath borne fiercely towards me. A jet of steam raised itself now and then to the level of my own floor. Ashes and cinders were falling freely around. The eruption was gathering strength as it went. It was dangerous any longer to lie so close to the broken edge. I must drag myself away, near the further precipice.

Frank would not return from town much before six, I felt sure. He always loitered when he got down to Hilo. Unless somebody came to relieve me soon I must surely be killed by slow torture.

I gazed all around me with a last despairing glance. As I did so, a cry of relief burst on a sudden from my parched throat. On the precipice above, leaning over the edge of the Floor of the Strangers, I saw distinctly a man's face, a man's face, a Hawaiian's as I thought, peering down curiously into the depths of the crater.

If only I could attract that man's attention I felt there might yet be some small chance for me.

CHAPTER V

The man was looking the other way. I must somehow manage to make him turn round to me.

I raised myself on my knees, put my hands to my mouth, and shouted aloud at the top of my voice, with the utmost force of which my lungs were capable. You never know how hard you can shout, till you've had to shout for dear life through a storm at sea, or some other terrible natural convulsion.

Could I make myself heard, I wondered to myself, above the constant hiss and roar and din of that volcanic outburst?

Thank Heaven, yes! The man turned and heard me. I could see him start and look sharply in the direction where I lay on the ledge. By the movement of his face I felt sure he observed me. He saw me and jumped back. He recognized the deadly peril in which I lay. "Help! help!" I shouted with terrific energy. "Quick! quick! a rope! The fire is almost upon me!"

The man rose and stood close to the brink. I could see by his dress quite clearly now that he was a native Hawaiian. Awe and surprise were visible on his face. He understood and drank in the full horror of my situation. Surely, surely, he would make haste to help me!

To my utter horror he did nothing of the sort. He stood still as if rooted to the spot in superstitious fear, and gazed down on my face with his own like a statue's. I never saw anything more stolid than his features, or the pose of his limbs. I flung up my arms appealingly for aid: I pointed with every gesture of pain and helplessness to my broken limb: I tried to express to him by natural pantomime the absolute necessity for immediate assistance. The native folded his arms in front and gazed placidly down with horrible unconcern in spite of my cries and shrieks and signs of agony. I knew now what it was to be a savage. He seemed utterly careless whether I lived or died. If I had been a worm or a scorpion or a venomous reptile he couldn't more wholly and totally have disregarded my obvious suffering.

At last, with the same look of indifference, he turned on his heel slowly, without one sign of encouragement, and disappeared from my sight towards the lip of the crater.

Had he gone to seek aid on my behalf, I wondered? Had he gone to call other natives to his assistance, and to bring ropes and ladders to haul me up from that unearthly crater?

I could not say, but I hardly dared hope it.

And all the while those billows of molten lava in the lake below surged madly on, rising and rising, and ever rising, tossing the wild fire-spray upon their angry crests, and making ready their greedy jagged teeth of flame as if on purpose to close on me and devour me piecemeal.

The volcano seemed indeed to be really alive. I didn't wonder the natives once saw in it a horrible, hungry, implacable goddess.

For ten minutes more I lay there still, half smothered by the sulphurous fumes of the rising gases, and whitened with a powdery shower of gray dust, waiting in agony for the inevitable end to arrive and stifle me. Then I looked up again, and saw to my surprise the native had come back to his former station. But not alone. Nor yet to save me. Three other Hawaiians, tall and shapely men, stood silent and moody by the first-comer's side, and gazed down as he had done, unmoved and unhorrified, upon myself and the crater.

Above the roar and crackling of the unquenchable fire, my ear, quickened by the straits in which I lay, caught just once the sound of the words they were saying. I had learnt a fair amount of Hawaiian since my arrival, and I could tell that in their talk "the anger of Pélé," "victim" and "stranger," occurred frequently. Could it be that they meant deliberately to leave me there unaided to die? Were they afraid to meddle with the prisoners of the goddess?

Christianized and civilized as they were in name, I knew too well then how deeply the old heathen superstitions must still be ingrained in the very core and fibre of their inmost being, not to fear that this might really be their hideous intention. The worship of Pélé might be dead, indeed, as a direct religion, but the awe and terror of Pélé's power I had long observed was as vivid and real in their hearts as ever. Even Kea herself, English as she was on her fathers side, half feared and propitiated that blood-thirsty goddess.

The four men drew slowly to the edge of the precipice. I couldn't hear, but I could see by their actions they were consulting together very earnestly. The heat by this time was growing intensely painful. I lifted up my hands and clasped them as if in prayer. After all, they were human. I trusted they might still be inclined to help me.

To my unspeakable terror, alarm, and dismay, the men shook their heads grimly in concert. Then all four of them, bowing down as if in worship towards the mouth of the crater, with their hands spread open in solemn accord, seemed to salute and adore the goddess of the volcano. I knew what it meant. I understood their gestures. Converts by profession as I doubt not they were, in their secret souls they were votaries of Pélé!

At that sight, I flung myself down on my side and gave up all for lost for ever. I thought of those who were nearest and dearest to me at home, and who would never behold my face again. I must die where I lay, unaided and unpitied.

When Frank returned to Kalaua's that night he would find no trace of me left on earth, not even a charred and blackened skeleton! The fire would have burnt me to fine gray ashes.

Presently, as I looked, a fifth man joined the group above, a man dressed as I had never before beheld any one. His head was covered with a huge shapeless mask, which seemed to me to represent a cruel grinning lace, with teeth and eyes of white mother-of-pearl, that glistened hideously in the ruddy glare of the fierce volcano. I had seen such a mask once in my life, I remembered well, before leaving England, in the ethnological room at the British Museum. That one, I knew, was made of rare Hawaiian red and yellow feathers, and was said to be used by the old heathen priests of cannibal days in offering up sacrifices to their blood-thirsty idols. The new-comer was further draped from head to foot in a long mantle of the same costly plumes, which concealed his limbs from view altogether. I don't know how, but I felt sure by the very way he moved across the ledge that the man with the mask was none other than Kalaua!

He was a priest of Pélé, then, to this very day! In spite of his outer veneer of civilization, in spite of his pretended conversion to a gentler creed, he still believed at heart in the vindictive and cruel goddess of the crater.

The man in the mask, walking slowly as in a solemn dance, approached the edge of the beetling precipice. The other four men grouped themselves around in set attitudes, two and two on either side of him. Their looks were impressive. The priest lifted up his hands slowly. His action as he lifted them, graceful yet majestic, convinced me more than ever that it was really Kalaua, I recognized the old chief's grim and stately statuesque air, the air as of a last surviving scion of the old man-eating Hawaiian nobility.

The priest stood still with his hands erect. The four others, in pairs on either side, bowed down their faces in awe to the ground. It was growing every moment more intolerably hot. I could scarcely watch them. The priest lifted up his voice aloud. I could catch not one word or syllable of what he said, but I was dimly aware in my intervals of pain that he was chanting some sort of measured savage litany. Every now and again he paused a moment, and then I could hear that his four companions answered him back in a solemn but loud response, in which I frequently fancied I caught the name of Pélé.

At that awful moment Kea's words came back distinctly to my mind. "The second ledge that you see down below there, in the dark glow, is the Floor of the Hawaiians: as far as that, only natives may penetrate. If a white man's foot ever treads that floor, Pélé will surely claim him for her victim. In the twinkling of an eye, like a feather in the flame, Pélé will shrivel him in her wrath to ashes."

I knew then what was happening up above. The priest of Pélé had come forth to the crater in his sacrificial garb, attended by his acolytes, and was performing a sort of dedicator death-service over Pélé's own chosen victim, before the flames rose up to embrace and devour me!

In spite of the heat, in spite of the pain, in spite of the bodily terror in which I lay and writhed, I remembered, too, what Kea had once told me, how in the old days when men sacrificed to Pélé they never burnt their offerings with earthly fire, but flung them whole, a living gift, into the cracks and fissures of the burning lava, that the goddess might consume her own victims for herself in her own unearthly subterranean furnaces!

It was an awful ceremony, yet surely an appropriate one.

The flames were rising nearer and nearer now. These cruel and hard-hearted men would do nothing to save me. I could see great jets of burning gas rise from time to time above the wall of the crater. I could hear the loud hiss and shiver of the unearthly steam. I could feel the hideous heat baking me slowly to death where I lay. I crossed my arms resignedly, and gave up all for lost. I would die at least at the post of honour, as an Englishman ought to die, without fear and without flinching. I only waited for the merciful flames to come and put me out of my lingering misery. It could not be long now I felt sure. The lava would soon flow fast all round me.

And above there, on the jagged edge of the precipice, the priest was still droning his terrible death-song, and the four tall men, bowed down to the ground almost, were still crying aloud in a strange monotone their hideous responses.

As the first few bubbles of boiling lava rose level at last with the top of the Floor of the Hawaiians, I caught the final words of their triumphant song. I knew what they meant; they were simple and easy. "Pélé has avenged herself on the WHITE MAN'S FOOT; the White Man's Foot that trod her floor; we offer up the white man's body in expiation to Pélé."

CHAPTER VI

While the ring of their heathen death-song still echoed in my ear, and the hiss and roar of the volcanic fires still boomed and resounded wildly around me, I was dimly conscious in an interval of heat that the lava-flood fell back for a few moments, and that a lull had intervened in that surging tide of fiery liquid. I was sorry for that. It would do nothing now but needlessly prolong my horrible torture. When once one has made up one's mind to face death, in whatever form, the sooner one can get the wrench over the better. To be roasted alive is bad enough in all conscience; but to be roasted alive by intermittent stages is a thing to make even a soldier or a man of science shrink back appalled from the ghastly prospect.

In my agony, I looked up once more at the sheer precipice. As I looked, I saw yet another person had come down to join the group by the edge. My heart bounded with a faint throb of hope. It was Kea, Kea, pretty, gentle Kea.

"Surely," I said to myself in my own soul, "Kea at least will not desert me. Kea will try her very best to save me."

The light of the volcano lit up the faces of the men and the girl with a ruddy glow. I could see every movement of their muscles distinctly. Kea came down with clasped hands, and blanched lips, like one frantic with terror, and seemed to beg and implore the man in the mask to aid or assist her in some projected undertaking. The man in the mask shook his head sternly. It was clear he was adamant. Kea redoubled her prayers and entreaties. The priest rejected her petition with his hands outspread, and turned once more as if in blind worship toward the mouth of the crater. I knew that Kea was begging hard for my life, and that Kalaua, sternly refusing her prayer, was devoting me as a victim to his unspeakable goddess.

There are moments that seem as long as years. This was one of them.

Presently, Kea seemed to ask some favour, some last favour. The stern old priest made answer slowly. I fancied he was relenting. She turned to the men, as if to ask a question. The men in return assented with a solemn movement of their awestruck bodies. Then Kea looked up at her uncle again imploringly. She spoke with fervour, I could see it was some sort of compact or bargain between them she was trying to negotiate. At last the man in the mask gave in. He nodded his head and folded his arms. He appeared to look on like a passive spectator. I imagined somehow, quickened as my senses were by the extremity of the moment, that he had entered into an agreement with her, not indeed to save me, but to abstain from active interference with Kea's movements if she wished herself to assist me in any way.

I breathed more freely. As soon as their hasty conference was over, the girl drew near to the brink of the precipice. She raised her hands as if pulling at an invisible rope: then she made signs to me to wait patiently, if wait I could, for that help was going to arrive shortly. After that, she broke eagerly away with a gesture of sympathy, and ran off in hot haste towards the winding path that led from the floor to the summit of the crater.

I lay there some minutes more in an agony of suspense. Would she come back in time, or would the fiery flood burst up once more to the level where I lay before she had time to arrive with assistance?

The man in the mask, whom I took to be Kalaua, and the four natives who stood by his side, still watched me, unmoved, with stolid indifference, from the jagged brink of that high granite precipice.

By and by, they looked down with deeper attention still. I could tell by their gestures and their excited manner that the lava, after its lull, had begun to ascend afresh. The man in the mask advanced and prostrated himself. He quivered with emotion. He flung his arms up wildly. His limbs shook. He seemed as if in the bodily presence of Pélé.

Next moment, a roar like the roar of thunder, or the discharge of a volley of heavy artillery, boomed forth from the crater, loud and sharp, with explosive violence. The ledge about me began to gape with chinks. Fissures opened up in the solid rock by my side with a crackling noise. The Floor of the Hawaiians sweated fire. Liquid lava oozed forth from a huge rent not three hundred yards away from the place where I lay, and flowing in a stream over the bed inward, fell back again in a surging cataract of fire into the central hollow. I wondered I was not scorched to death outright, so near was the lava-flood. But the place where I lay still remained solid. How long it would remain so, I did not even dare to speculate.

At that instant, as I looked up in my agony of suspense towards the brink of the precipice, with the liquid fire rising apace to seize me, I saw Kea, all breathless with haste, rush eagerly up to the edge and lean over towards me. In her hands, O joy, she held a large coil or ring of something. Thank heaven! Thank heaven! My heart bounded with delight. Saved! saved! It was rope she was carrying!

She flung it down in a curl, sailor-fashion, towards the spot where I lay. I saw as it fell it was of different sizes, and knotted together with big rude knots in many places. Clearly she had not been able to find a single rope long enough for her purpose. She had made up this length as well as she was able out of different pieces hunted up by hazard in odd corners at Kalaua's on the spur of the moment.

It was a giddy height to which to trust one's self, even with the stoutest and strongest cable ever woven on earth. But with that weak and patched-up line of rotten old cords? Impossible! Impossible! If one of the knots were to give way with my weight, if one of the pieces were to break in the middle, I should be hurled down again a second time, yet more helpless than ever, and dashed into little pieces in an instant on that sharp and stubborn granite platform!

But drowning men clutch at straws. This was no moment to deliberate or reason. I would have trusted myself just then, broken leg and all, to a line of whipcord, if nothing else came handy.

The rope descended in a whirl through the air. It fell taut, plumb to the bottom. A fresh disappointment! To my utter horror, the end still dangled some ten feet above me!

I couldn't possibly jump up to reach it. With a loud cry of distress Kea saw it was too short. In a moment without stopping to think or hesitate, she had torn the lower part of her long native dress into strips and shreds, and lengthened the frail cord by this insecure addition just far enough to reach me as I stood on tip-toe.

I clutched it at last with both my hands, and threw back my head as a signal to Kea that all was right, and she might begin pulling.

Never shall I forget the awful sensations that coursed through my body as I dangled there, half-way in air, while that delicate young girl, thin and graceful, but strong of limb, with the inherited strength of her savage country-women, hauled me slowly up by main force of struggling nerve and sinew, past all possible conception of her natural powers.

She hauled me up by first passing the rope round a jagged peak of lava, which thus acted as a sort of rude natural pulley, enabling her to get rid of the direct strain, and to throw the weight in part on the edge of the precipice, and then by winding it round her own waist as a living windlass. Slowly, slowly, clinging by my hands to the hard rope, that cut and bruised my poor bleeding fingers, and with my broken leg dangling painfully in mid-air with excruciating twitches, I rose by degrees towards the brink of the abyss. How Kea had ever strength to raise me I do not know to this very day. I only know that as each knot on the rope grated and jerked round the edge of the peak that served for pulley it sent a thrill of incredible and unutterable pain through my injured limb, and almost made me let go my hands off the hard rope they were grasping and clutching with all their energy.

Meanwhile, the man in the feather mask and the natives by his side stood stolidly by, neither helping nor hindering, but gazing at me as I dangled in mid-air with sublime indifference, as one might gaze at a spider running up his own web with practised feet towards his nest on the ceiling. It was clear my life was no more to them than that. If the rope had given way, if the crumbling peak of honey-combed lava had broken short with the weight, and precipitated me, a mangled mass, to the bottom, they would have stood there as stolidly, and smiled as imperturbably at my shattered limbs in the awful embrace of their fiery goddess. Truly, truly, the dark places of the earth are full of cruelty.

As I rose in the air the lava, now belching forth with renewed vigour, followed me fast up the mouth of the crater. It followed me fast, like a living creature. One might almost have fancied that Pélé, disappointed of her victim, made haste in her frantic efforts to snatch him from the hands of that frail mortal maiden who strove almost in vain to rescue him in time by violent means from her cruel clutches. I didn't wonder any longer that those ignorant and superstitious natives should picture the volcano to themselves in their own souls as a living will. I almost felt it alive myself, so wildly and eagerly did the tongues of flame seem to dart forth towards me with their forked and vibrating tips, as if thirsting to lick me up and swallow me down in their hungry lunges.

The time I took in rising was endless. Could I hold on till the end? that was the question. At last, after long intervals of giddy suspense, I reached the top, or almost reached it; I clutched the crumbling peak with my hooked fingers. Kea still wound the rope round and round her body, as she approached to help me. She held out her hand. I grasped it eagerly. "You must jump," she cried: and all wounded as I was, I jumped with wild force on to the solid floor of the upper platform. My broken leg thrilled through with pain. But I was safe, safe. I was standing by her side on the Floor of the Strangers. The lava sank down again with a hideous sob, as if disappointed of its living prey. I gazed around me for the priest and his acolytes. Not a sign or a mark of them anywhere was to be seen. I stood alone with Kea by the brink of the precipice. The rest had melted away to their hidden lairs as if by magic.

I was rescued, indeed, but by the skin of my teeth. Such peril leaves one unmanned as one escapes it.

CHAPTER VII

I couldn't walk with my broken leg. My gentle preserver took me up in her arms with tender care, and lifted me, strong man as I am, bodily from the ground as if I had been a week-old baby. It was partly her powerful Hawaiian limbs and sinews that did it no doubt, but still more, I believe, that wonderful nervous energy with which Nature supplies even the weakest of our kind when they stand face to face at last in some painful crisis with a great emergency.

She carried me slowly up the zig-zag path, and over the lip of the crater to Kalaua's house. Then she laid me down to rest upon a bamboo bed, and went out to fetch me food and water.

What happened next I hardly knew, for once on the bed, I fainted immediately with pain and exhaustion.

When I next felt conscious, it was well on in the night. I found myself stretched at full length on the bed, with Frank leaning over me in brotherly affection, and an American doctor, hastily summoned from Hilo, endeavouring to restore me by all the means in his power.

At the foot stood Kalaua, no longer grim and severe as formerly, but, much to my surprise, the very picture of intelligent and friendly sympathy.

"How did you get here so soon?" I asked the doctor, when I was first able to converse with him rationally. "You must have hurried up very fast from Hilo."

"I did," he answered, going on with his work uninterruptedly. "Your friend Kalaua fetched me up.

"He happened to be here when that brave girl rescued you from the crater, and he rode down on one of his little mountain ponies in the quickest time I ever remember to have known made between Hilo and the summit. He was extremely anxious I should get back quickly to see you at once, and we cantered up on the return journey as I never before cantered in the whole course of my life. I've nearly broken my own bones, I can tell you, in my haste and anxiety to set yours right for you."

"That's very good of you," I answered gratefully.

"Oh! you needn't thank me for it," he replied, with a laugh. "It was all our good friend Kalaua's doing. He wouldn't even allow me to draw rein for a moment till I halted at last beside his own verandah."

I gazed at Kalaua in the blankest astonishment. Could it really be he who had stood so stolidly by in the feather mask and devoted my head with awful rites to the nether gods while I lay helpless on the Floor of the Hawaiians? My confidence in his identity began distinctly to waver. After all, I hadn't seen the features of that grim heathen priest while I lay at the bottom. Perhaps I was mistaken. He was Kea's uncle. For Kea's sake, I ardently hoped so.

They set my leg that very night, and Frank and Kalaua in turns sat up to nurse me. I can hardly say which of the two was kinder or tenderer. Kalaua watched me, indeed, as a woman watches by her son's bedside. He was ready with drink, or food, or medicine, whenever I wanted it. His wakeful eyelids never closed for a moment. No mother could have tended her own child more patiently.

"Is the volcano still at work, Frank?" I asked once, in a painless interval. I could never forget, even on a sick bed, that I was by trade a man of science.

"No, my dear old fellow," Frank answered affectionately. "The volcano, finding you were no longer in a fit condition to observe it, has politely retired to the deepest recesses of its own home till you're in a proper state to continue your investigations. The moment you were safely out of the hole, Kea tells me, it sank back like a calm sea to its usual level."

"Pélé is satisfied," the old man muttered to himself in Hawaiian from the bottom of the bed, not thinking I understood him. "She has given up her claim to the victim who offered himself of his own accord upon her living altar."

It was not till next morning that I saw Kea again. The poor girl was pale and evidently troubled. She received all my expressions of gratitude with a distracted air, and she hardly appeared at times to be quite conscious of what was passing around her. But she was gentle and considerate and kind as ever, even more kind, I fancied, than we had yet known her.

For the next week, Frank, Kalaua, and Kea in turn each bore their fair share in nursing and watching me. I wondered to myself, after all that had happened, that I wasn't afraid of stopping any longer under the old chief's roof; yet now that it was all over, my staying there for the time seemed somehow quite natural. Indeed, it would have been impossible to carry me further along the rugged road that led down the mountain, with my leg in splints, and my general health in a most enfeebled condition. And I wasn't in the least afraid, either that Kalaua would cut my throat in his own house, or otherwise offer me personal violence. Nothing could possibly exceed his personal kindness to me now: and I felt as safe in the old chief's hands as I did in his niece's, or in my own brother's.

My conversations with the American doctor too reassured me greatly in this curious matter. A day or two later, I told him the whole strange and romantic story, in far fuller detail than I have told it here (for all the incidents were then fresh in my memory), and he listened with the air of a man to whom such marvellous recitals of savage superstition were hardly anything out of the common.

"I shouldn't be surprised if it really was Kalaua," he said to me confidentially, when I had finished my narrative. "The fact is, the old man has always been more or less suspected of persistent Pélé worship. Beliefs like that don't die out in a single generation. But you needn't be afraid on that account that he'll do you any bodily harm now. Pélé cares nothing for unwilling victims. She takes those only who go to her willingly. You fell in of yourself, and therefore Kalaua wouldn't pull you out. To have done so would have been to incur the severest wrath of Pélé. But now that you've once got safe out again, every good old-fashioned heathen Hawaiian will hold to it as a cardinal article of faith, that you're absolutely inviolable. The goddess had you once in her power, and of her own free will she has let you go again. If she liked, she might have eaten you, but she let you go. That shows you are one for whom she has a special concern and regard. The moment you got up in safety to the brink once more, the lava fell back. To Kalaua, that would be a certain sign and token that Pélé relinquished all claim upon your body. She may take some other victim, unawares, in your stead: but you yourself, the Hawaiians believe, are henceforth and forever next door to invulnerable. You are Taboo to Pélé."

"Well, I've been very nearly dipped in Styx," I answered, smiling, "so I ought to be inviolable. But you don't think, then, I run any risk by remaining under this roof till my leg gets well again?"

"Quite the contrary," the doctor replied with perfect confidence. "I should think you would nowhere be treated with greater care, consideration, and courtesy than here at Kalaua's. Whatever it may have been a very few days ago, these people regard you now as Pélé's favourite. If you were to ask politely for a White Elephant, they'd import one for you direct, I verily believe, by the first mail steamer in from Burmah."

"That's lucky," I said, "though after what I saw in the crater the other day, I confess I feel a little nervous at times about our personal safety."

As the doctor was just taking his leave, he turned and said to me in a very serious tone, "If I were you, do you know, Mr. Hesselgrave, I think I wouldn't say anything at all in public while you remain in Hawaii about the scene in the crater."

"No?" I said interrogatively.

"No," he answered. "You see, it's impossible to prove anything. After all, when one looks the thing squarely in the face, what did you really see and feel sure of? Why, just five natives looking down at you in the crater, on the very eve of a serious outbreak of the volcano. Well, nobody's bound to risk his life to rescue a stranger from the jaws of an eruption. As to the mask, the less said about that the better. People won't believe you: they'll say it's impossible. I believe you, because I understand Hawaiians down to the very ground: I know how skin-deep their civilization goes: but folks who don't, will think you're romancing. Besides, Kalaua wouldn't like it, of course. It's bad form to be a heathen in Hawaii. Whatever the natives may be in their own hearts, in their outer lives they prefer to be considered civilized Christians. There's nothing riles your true-born Hawaiian like a public imputation of cannibalism or heathendom."

"All right," I answered. "You may depend upon my discretion," For Kea's sake indeed I should have been sorry to bring disgrace upon her stern old uncle, however richly the old chief might have merited it. I was profoundly grateful to her for her gallant rescue; it would have been an ill reward indeed to repay her kindness by betraying the terrible secret of her family.

CHAPTER VIII

All that night Kea sat up with me; and somewhat to my surprise she occupied herself for most of the time in working at a great white veil of very fine material.

"That looks like a bridal veil, Kea," I said at last, regarding it curiously in an interval of sleeplessness.

Kea laughed, not merrily as heretofore, but a very sad laugh. "It is a bridal veil," she answered, blushing and stammering. "I—I'm working at it at present for—for one of my family."

I saw she was embarrassed, so I asked her no further questions about it. Perhaps, I thought, she's going to be married. Even in Polynesia, young girls are naturally reticent upon that subject. And Kea was hardly a Polynesian at all: on her father's side she was an English lady. So I turned on my back and dismissed the matter for the moment from my consideration.

For eight long weary weeks I lay there on my bed, or on the adjoining sofa, with my leg slowly and tediously healing, and my head much bothered by such long inaction. What made me more impatient still of my enforced idleness was the fact that, according to Frank's continuous report, Mauna Loa was now rumbling, and grumbling, and mumbling away in a more persistently threatening style than ever. I was afraid there was going to be a really grand eruption on the large scale, and that I wouldn't be well enough to be there to observe it. It would be ignominious indeed for the accredited representative of the British Association for the Advancement of Science to be carried down the mountain on a hospital stretcher at the very moment when perhaps the finest volcanic display of the present century was just about to inaugurate its arrival by a magnificent outburst of lava and ashes. I should feel like a soldier who turned his back upon the field of battle: like a sailor who went below to the ladies' cabin at the first approach of a West Indian hurricane.

The idea distressed me and gnawed my heart out. If you are a man of science you will understand and sympathize with me. If you are not, you will perhaps consider me a donkey.

Kalaua meanwhile remained as courteous and attentive as ever. But he often came in from the mountain much perturbed in soul, as I could see by his manner, and as I gathered, also, from his remarks to Kea. I understood Hawaiian pretty well by this time. I'm naturally quick at languages, I believe, and I've travelled about the world so much, in search of the playful and pensive volcano, that a new idiom comes to me readily: and besides, I had nothing to do while I lay idle on my bed but to take lessons in the native dialect from Kea. Now a pretty girl, it is well known, is the best possible teacher of languages. You understand at once from her mouth what you would only vaguely guess at on a man and a brother's. You read from her eyes what her lips are saying.

"Pélé's uneasy again, my niece," the old man would murmur often as he entered. "I never knew the crater more disturbed. Pélé is angry. She will flood Hawaii. She will drown the people. We must try to quiet her."

Kea looked down always when he spoke like that with a guilty look upon her poor young face. I understood that look. I knew she considered she had cheated the goddess by rescuing me from the flames, and I grieved to think that I should cause her unhappiness.

"Kea," I said to her one day, as she sat still sewing away at a pure white dress in the room by my side, "do you know anything of your English relations, your father's people?"

Kea burst suddenly into a flood of tears. "I wish I did!" she cried earnestly. "I wish I could go to them. I wish I could get away from Hawaii for ever. I'm tired of this terrible, terrible island. It wears my heart out." And she flung away the dress from her in an agony of horror, and fled from the room, still crying bitterly.

"I see what it is," I said to myself pityingly. "They want to marry that helpless young girl to somebody or other she doesn't like. Probably a fat old native with a good thing in cocoa-nuts and sugar-plantations. Poor child! I can easily understand her feelings. She, an English girl almost, in blood and sentiment, to be tied to some wretched old Hawaiian ex-cannibal, some creature incapable of appreciating or sympathizing with her! I don't wonder she shrinks from the horrid prospect. She's a great deal too good and too sweet for any of them."

I may mention however, to prevent misconception, that I was not myself the least little bit in the world in love with Kea. I merely regarded her from a brotherly point of view, with friendship and gratitude. The fact is, a certain young lady in a remote English country rectory, who received a letter from me by every Honolulu mail regularly, might have had just ground of complaint against me had I harboured any trace of such a feeling in my heart towards the gentle little Hawaiian maiden. It was the thought of that particular English lady that caused me so much agony as I lay on the floor of Mauna Loa that awful morning. Nothing else could have made me cling to the last chance of life with so fierce a clinging. For my own part, as a man of science, I have rather a contempt for any fellow who will not willingly risk his own neck, under ordinary circumstances, for any great or noble cause on which he may be occupied: and among such great and noble causes I venture to hold the pursuit of truth and natural knowledge by no means inferior to the pursuit of liberty or of material welfare. But when there's a lady in the case, why, then, of course, the case is altered. A man must then, to some extent, consult his own personal safety. His life is not entirely his own to lose: he has mortgaged it as it were on behalf of another. This however is a pure digression, for which I must apologize, on the ground that it is needful to prevent misapprehension of the relation in which I stood to Kea. Forgive me for thus for a moment dragging in my own private and domestic feelings.

In a few minutes Kea returned again. She had an envelope with a name and address on it in her hand. She gave it to me simply. Her eyes were still red with crying. "That's where my father's people live," she said quietly. "I wish I was with them. My father wanted me to return to them when he died. But I was afraid to go, because—because, though they asked me after his death, they never wrote to me while he was alive, they never wrote to him either, They were angry with him for marrying my mother."

She said it with infinite tenderness and regret. I glanced at the address Kea had given me, and saw to my surprise the name of her father's brother, he was a clergyman in Kent, well known, as it happened, to my own family in England.

"I wish you could go to them, Kea," I cried earnestly. "Whatever they think and feel now, they couldn't help liking you and loving you when they saw you. I wish you could get away from this dreadful Hawaii!"

"I wish I could," Kea answered in a hopeless voice. "But—" she paused for a moment. "I must stop here now; I must stop here, till my marriage!"

She pointed to the white dress that lay huddled upon the floor; and, with the tears welling up into her eyes once more, rushed madly and desperately out of the room like one distracted.

I couldn't help contrasting the life of that peaceful Kentish rectory with the awful surroundings of the priest of Pélé, and wishing I could rescue that gentle girl from so terrible a place, as she herself had rescued me from the floor of Mauna Loa.

And I wondered to myself to whom on earth they could ever mean against her will to marry her.

Meanwhile, in spite of my broken leg, the volcano itself attracted no little share of my distinguished attention. I couldn't go out to call on it in person, to be sure; but I had in Frank an acute and well-trained assistant, who could be trusted to keep a steady eye upon its daily proceedings, and who knew exactly what traits in its character I wished him to report to me. In order that I might the more fully be kept informed from time to time of the state of the crater, and the momentary changes taking place in its temper and the lava level, I taught Frank in his leisure moments how to work a heliograph. For that purpose I fastened a slanting piece of looking-glass to my own bed-head, and stationed my brother with a second mirror on the summit of the mountain, in a good position for observing the lake of fire and the smoke-stacks in its centre. On this simple form of telegraphic arrangement Frank flashed me news by the Morse code; so many long and short flashes in certain fixed and regular orders standing each for a certain letter: and I flashed him back by the same method my directions and remarks on his own despatches. In this way we constantly kept up quite a brisk conversation by means of the mirrors. "Lava now rising in the main basin;" Frank would flash over to me. "Any fissures?" I would ask. In a minute the answer came promptly back, "Yes, two, in the black basalt." "Steam issuing from them?" "None at present, but clouds of dense smoke forming slowly in the second cavern." "All right: then note its volume and direction." And so forth for an hour at a time together. It relieved the monotony of my existence on my sick bed thus to carry on by proxy my accustomed avocations: and I was glad to feel I wasn't quite useless, even with my broken leg to weigh me down, but was honestly earning my bread (or at least my taro-paste) from the subscribers to the British Association Seismological Committee Fund.

One evening, towards the end of my convalescence, Frank came in in very high spirits (for Mauna Loa had been smoking like a German student that day) and found Kea busy as usual at her endless task of making her own very extensive trousseau. She was at work now on a long white satin train, which certainly seemed to me far more expensive and handsome in texture and quality than I should ever have expected a Hawaiian half caste girl to wear for her wedding.

"What a swell you are, Kea!" Frank cried, half chaffingly. "I wonder what sort of a match you expect to make, that you're getting yourself up so smart for the occasion?"

Kea glanced back at him with a painfully sad and serious face. "I'm going to marry a very important personage indeed," she said solemnly.

"A chief, perhaps?" Frank suggested laughing, and peeling a banana.

The tears stood in poor Kea's eyes, though Frank did not notice them. "Higher than a chief," she answered slowly, with a deep-drawn sigh.

"A prince of the blood-royal of Hawaii, then," Frank went on, boy-like, without observing how serious and painful the conversation seemed to the poor little half-caste.

"Higher than a prince," Kea replied once more almost reverently.

"What! Not the King!" Frank exclaimed in astonishment.

"The King is married already," Kea replied with dignity, the tears trickling one by one down her cheeks, unseen by Frank, who, busy with his banana, couldn't observe her downcast face as well as I could from my place on the pillow.

"Higher than a chief! Higher than a prince! Higher than the King!" Frank cried incredulously. "Hang it all, Kea; why, then, you must be going to marry the captain of an American whaler!"

I laughed in spite of myself. Hawaiian royalty, to say the truth, when you see it on the spot (as we had done at Honolulu) is such a very cheap sort of imitation kingship! But Kea, instead of laughing, burst suddenly into tears, and flung down her work on the floor in an agony of despondency. "Frank," I cried, "how on earth can you tease her so? Don't you see poor Kea's dreadfully distressed? It's downright cruelty to chaff on such a subject."

Kea turned her big brown eyes full upon me, all tearful as they were. "If you knew all," she answered, "you would say so indeed. You would pity me, both of you, oh, how you would pity me!"

And without another word, she rose like a queen and glided from the room, muttering to herself some inaudible sentence in Hawaiian as she retreated.

When she had left us alone, Frank turned to me, abashed, with unusual earnestness and wonder in his voice. "Tom," said he impressively, "does it ever strike you there's something very mysterious indeed about this marriage of Kea's?"

"How so?" I asked; though in fact I felt it quite as much as he did, but I wanted to hear Frank's own unadulterated idea about the matter.

"Why, you see," he answered, "they're getting ready for a wedding: but where's the bridegroom? A marriage is never quite complete without a man in the proceedings. Now, we've never seen any young man come courting around; especially not any one so very important as Kea makes her future husband out to be. A bridegroom, I take it, is an indispensable sort of accompaniment to every respectable civilized wedding. You can't very well get on without him. But he's not forthcoming here. It seems to me there's something awfully uncanny about it all."

"I often hear them speak among themselves," I said, "about somebody called Maloka. I wonder who on earth this Maloka is? I expect it's Maloka she's going to marry."

"I'll make inquiries," Frank answered decisively. "We must get to the bottom of it. For my part, Tom I don't half like the look of it."

CHAPTER IX

That night I hardly closed my eyes in sleep. My leg, which for several days had scarcely pained me, became troublesome once more with a sort of violent twitching neuralgic rheumatism. Never before had I felt anything so curiously spasmodic. I had tossed about during the evening indeed a great deal more than usual, and Kalaua, who noted my discomfort with his keen and observant Hawaiian glance, asked me more than once how I felt, with apparent kindliness. I told him my symptoms in perfect frankness. "Aha," he cried grimly, looking back at me with a smile. "That settles the matter. We shall have an eruption then. The old-time folk in heathen days always noticed that all neuralgic and rheumatic pains became far more severe when an eruption was brewing."

"Did they?" I answered languidly; "that was no doubt a mere heathen superstition on their part."

"Oh, no," he retorted with flashing eyes: "it was no superstition. It was solemn fact. Wounds would never heal at such times, and broken limbs would set with difficulty. You see, in the old clays, we knew a good deal about wounds, of course, far more than nowadays. We were all warriors then. We fought and hacked each other. We were often liable to get severely injured. Stone hatchets cut a man up so awkwardly."

"Why," I cried, "now you come to mention it, I remember the year I was working at Etna, the Sicilians at Catania all declared that sprains and cuts and rheumatic affections would never get well before or during eruptive periods. I hardly believed them at the time, I confess; but if two people so widely apart in race and space as you and the Sicilians both say so, I dare say there may really be something in it."

"There is something in it," Kalaua echoed gravely. "I know it by experience."

"An atmospheric or electric condition, no doubt," I said, lighting a cigarette.

"Our fathers used to think," Kalaua corrected slowly, "that Pélé's daughter was the goddess of disease; and when Pélé was angrily searching for a victim, or when Pélé's son, the humpbacked god, who lives with his mother among the ashes of the crater, was in search of a fresh wife among the daughters of men, then, our heathen forefathers used to say, the goddess of disease went forth through the land to prick the people with the goads and thorns that she pushed into their flesh and their veins and their marrow. Pélé had many sons and daughters; all of them worked the will of their mother. The goddess of disease was the eldest and noblest, she searched everywhere for a victim for her mother."

"And did she ever get one?" I asked with curdling blood.

"Yes," Kalaua answered. "The Hawaiians are brave. Sometimes the people would suffer so much from Pélé's daughter that someone among them, a noble-minded youth, would willingly offer himself up as a propitiation to Pélé. Then Pélé's wrath would be appeased for the time, and the eruptions would cease, and the land would have slumber. But those, we know, were only foolish old heathen ideas. Nowadays of course the Hawaiians are wiser.

"Yes," I replied, smiling and withdrawing my cigarette. "The Hawaiians nowadays are nominally Christian."

The phrase seemed to excite Kalaua's suspicions. "We know now," he went on more quietly, with a searching look, "that eruptions are due to purely natural causes."

"I hope," I said, "if an eruption's coming, I shall be well enough anyhow to get out and watch it. The doctor promised soon to let me have a pair of crutches."

Kalaua smiled. "If an eruption comes at all," he answered, with the air of a man who speaks of what he knows, "it'll come, I take it, on Saturday next, and you won't be well enough to get out by then. The moon will be full on Saturday at midnight. Eruptions come oftenest at the full moon. Our fathers had a foolish old reason for that, they said that Pélé and her son had a grudge against the moon, and strove always to put it out with their belching fire, for eclipses, they thought in their ignorance and folly, were caused by Pélé's humpbacked son trying to strangle the moon in its cradle."

"Why," I said, "that's likely enough, when one comes to think of it."

Kalaua gazed at me in speechless amazement. "That Pélé's son is the cause of eclipses!" he cried, astonished.

"No, no," I answered. "No such nonsense as that. But the connection may be real between phases of the moon and volcanic phenomena. The moon's attraction must be just as powerful on the lava in a volcano as on the water in the sea. There may be a sort of spring-tide tendency towards eruptions so to speak. And curiously enough, since you mention eclipses, there's going to be an eclipse of the moon on Saturday."

Kalaua's face changed suddenly at the word. "An eclipse!" he cried, with intense solemnity. "An eclipse of the moon! On Saturday!—impossible!"

"No, not impossible," I said. "I see it by the almanac."

"Not total?" Kalaua asked excitedly.

"Yes, total." I answered, amused at his excitement. "You think that will bring an eruption in its train?"

"Eclipses always bring eruptions," Kalaua said solemnly. "Our fathers told us so, and we ourselves have proved it."

"Well, you may be right:" I replied smiling; "we really know so little about these things as yet that it's impossible to dogmatize in any particular instance. But for my own part, I believe there's no counting upon eruptions. Sometimes they come and sometimes they don't! They're like the weather, exactly like the weather, products of pure law, yet wholly unaccountable."

Kalaua rose width great resolution. "An eclipse of the moon!" he repeated to himself aloud in Hawaiian. "Kea, Kea, come here and listen! An eclipse on Saturday! How very strange, Kea! That's earlier than any of us at all expected. How lucky we made our arrangements so well beforehand, or else this thing might have taken us all quite unprepared. There'll be an eruption. We must look out for that! I must go at once and tell Maloka!"

Maloka, then, the mysterious bridegroom, lived quite near! Kalaua could go out at a minute's notice, and speak to him easily. I longed to ask him who Maloka was, where he lived, and what he did, but a certain sense of shame and propriety restrained me. After all, Kalaua was my host. I had no business to go prying into the private affairs of a native family who had been kind enough to extend to me their friendly hospitality.

Kalaua left the room and went out hurriedly. I turned on my bed and tried to sleep. But try as I would, my leg still kept me persistently awake. Frank was soon snoring soundly in his own room next door. I envied him his rest, and gave myself up to a sleepless night with what resignation I could manage to summon.

Gradually, as the night wore on I began to doze. A numb drowsiness stole slowly over me. I almost slept, I fancy; at any rate, I closed my eyes and ceased to think about anything in particular. For half an hour I was practically unconscious. Then on a sudden, as I lay there dozing, a slight noise attracted my attention. I opened my eyes and stared out silently. The door of my bedroom was pushed gently open. A hand held it gingerly ajar for a while. A brown head was thrust in at the slit, and then another. "Softly!" a voice murmured low in Hawaiian. I lay still, and never moved a thread or muscle of my face, but gazing across dimly through my closed eyelids I could see that one of the men was Kalaua; the other, I imagined, was a perfect stranger. My heart beat fast. Strange thoughts thronged me. "Surely," I said to myself, "this must be Maloka."

I was dying with curiosity to learn something more about that unknown bridegroom. But I dared not move. I dared not speak. A solemn awe seemed to thrill and overcome me.

"Is he asleep?" the stranger asked in a low voice.

"Yes, fast asleep," Kalaua replied in Hawaiian. "Can he understand if he hears?" the stranger said again.

"Not much, if anything," Kalaua answered. "He has only been such a short time in Hawaii."

I was glad they under-estimated my knowledge of their language. It enabled me to learn what they were talking about.

"Then we can speak with safety," the stranger went on.

Kalaua nodded, went out once more, and closed the door softly behind him. They both seated themselves as far as I could guess, on chairs in the sitting-room. Oh, how I longed to hear the rest of their conversation! It was quite irresistible. Curiosity got the better of my native prudence. I couldn't catch a word of what they were saying with any distinctness where I lay on the bed. I must rise and listen. I undid the splints that bound up my leg; crawled carefully across the room without jerking or hurting it; and throwing myself down at the bedroom door, bent eagerly though cautiously down to the key-hole.

Even so, I could catch but little.

Kalaua and the stranger were conversing in low and earnest tones in their native language. Though I could understand Hawaiian pretty well by this time, I found it hard to follow so rapid and familiar a colloquy between two Hawaiians in half-whispered accents.

They spoke of many things I didn't understand. But one thing I was sure I caught from time to time quite distinctly, and that was the oft-repeated name, Maloka. They were talking of Maloka, Maloka, Maloka. Was this Maloka? I asked myself more than once. If so, I should like to take a good look at the man who has to be Kea's future husband.

Why all this mystery? This midnight meeting? Why couldn't Kea be quietly married like any one else? Why couldn't Kea's lover come to the house at a reasonable hour, like all the rest of humanity? I must clear up this question, one way or the other. It was very wrong of me, no doubt; but in my anxiety to learn the whole truth of the case, I held my eye for a second to the key-hole. The stranger's face was turned towards me now. I recognized him in a moment. He was one of the four tall, stately natives who had stood by Kalaua's side on the brink of the precipice that awful day when Kea rescued me. This, then, was Maloka!

My blood ran cold. Kea married to this cold stern creature!

But no. A minute later I caught their words once more. The stranger himself was speaking this time. "And you went down and told Maloka exactly when and where to expect her?" he asked seriously.

"Yes," Kalaua answered. "It's all arranged. I told Maloka. I went out at once to see him and to tell him."

A sudden thrill passed through me irresistibly. Wrong again. This, then, was not Maloka after all! But Maloka, whoever he was, lived quite near. It had taken Kalaua only half an hour or so apparently to go to his house and tell him the story of the expected eruption.

"She may well be honoured," the stranger murmured. "So great a marriage is indeed an honour to any girl in Hawaii."

They whispered together for a few minutes longer in a lower voice, even more mysteriously, but I could catch very little of all they said, except that now and then the words "marriage," "bridegroom," "bride," and "distinction" fell upon my ears quite unmistakably. Once, to my surprise, my own name, too, came into their colloquy. I strained my ears to catch the meaning. They repeated it once more. Strange! I couldn't quite understand what they meant, but I seemed to be somehow mixed up with the mystery. Was this, could it be, some wonderful heathen plot or contrivance to carry me off and marry me perforce against my will to Kea?

"She rescued him," I heard Kalaua say in a very stern tone: the next words I couldn't quite catch, then he added more distinctly, "and she must marry him."

"It is the law of our forefathers," the strange Hawaiian repeated. "Life for life. Bride for husband."

"For fifty years have I served faithfully," Kalaua said, "and now I may surely be honoured in the marriages of my family."

"Good," the other man answered. "You will see to the bride; and I for my part will take every care that the bridegroom is ready."

"Don't fear for me," Kalaua replied. "The daughters of the Hawaiians shrink not from their duty."

He rose, and walked across the room in the opposite direction from that of the door where I still sat crouching on the ground in my night-shirt, with my broken leg extended sideways in front of me. He went up to the wall and pushed aside a picture that hung from a nail near the ceiling before me. Behind it was a small brass knob. He took a little key from his pocket, which he fitted into the midst of the knob, and suddenly, with a spring a door opened. It was the door of a cupboard or small recess let into the wall, and in it I saw for the twinkling of an eye an apparition of something brilliantly red and yellow. I knew in a second what that thing was. It was the royal robe of sacred feathers that Kalaua had worn as his priest's costume when he solemnly dedicated me to the anger of Pélé.

Behind it, two horrible goggle eyes shone forth with lurid gleams into the blank room. I knew those too, they were the eyes of the mask, that grinning mask that Kalaua wore as the sign of his priestship.

Hideous, barbaric, staring things; but Kalaua regarded them with the utmost veneration.

"Everything is correct," he whispered, looking over the strange paraphernalia with a stern look of content and handling them reverently. "The wedding shall come off, then, duly as arranged. We know the place, the day, and the hour. I answer for the bride: you answer for the bridegroom. All is well. It is an auspicious marriage. May they live happily ever after!"

"Such is the prayer of all the Hawaiians," the stranger answered, with the air of a man who recites some liturgy.

Kalaua bowed his head solemnly. "Among the faithless," he said, "we at least are faithful."

He shut the door once more, and locked it securely. Then he turned towards the room where I was eagerly watching him through that narrow key-hole. How I knew what was coming next I can never tell, but I did know somehow that they were moving across once more to my hiding place. Fear supplied me with strength and agility. Dragging my leg after me again with breathless haste, I managed to scramble back into my bed somehow, and, pulling the sheet over me, to feign sleep, before those two savage devotees of a dead religion were once more leaning over the pillow beside me. Next instant, I heard the door pushed cautiously open a second time; and peering afresh through my closed eyelids, I saw Kalaua and his nameless satellite steal over softly to where I lay half dead with terror and excitement.

I closed my eyes and waited, awestruck.

Were they really come to murder me or to carry me off by force? Were they going to marry me against my will to Kea? Did Kalaua mean to put me there and then through some hideous and inhuman wedding ceremony? Was I the bridegroom for whom the stranger was to answer? Was this the secret of their sudden kindness to me? Was I bound to atone for the saving of my life by accepting in wedlock the last daughter and heiress of the priests of Pélé?

But no! My suspicions must surely be wrong. It was Maloka, Maloka, that unknown Maloka, who was destined to be the simple little brown maiden's hated bridegroom. I must find out soon who Maloka was; but for the moment, fear got the better of curiosity.

The two Hawaiians approached on tiptoe to my side. My heart beat hard, but I gave no token. I lay as still as death, and breathed heavily. I felt rather than heard them stoop down and look at me.

"Asleep?" asked the stranger.

"Asleep!" Kalaua answered.

"Let us see!" the stranger said, and moved his robe a little. I knew he had drawn a knife from his girdle. I felt him raise it but I never cringed.

There was a moment's suspense, an awful suspense, for I didn't feel sure they hadn't come to murder me, and then, apparently satisfied, the men withdrew; the footsteps retreated as stealthily as they had approached; and the door was closed again noiselessly behind them.

They had only come, after all, to make sure I was asleep and had heard nothing. Whatever this business might be on which they were engaged, they evidently meant to conduct it with the utmost secrecy. Whatever these things meant, they did not mean murder.

CHAPTER X

Next morning, as I lay on the sofa in the verandah, humming and idling, with Kea still stitching away at the very last touches on her wedding garments beside me, I saw by a sudden glitter in my mirror that Frank was anxious to heliograph me a message. Pulling the cord that moved my looking-glass, I flashed back "Well?" Frank answered by signal, "Big ship off Hilo. Gunboat apparently. Flying British colours. A party is landing."

I signalled back by code, "Try to attract their attention if possible, and ask them what's their business in Hawaii."

For a few minutes Frank seemed engaged in establishing communications with the newly-arrived gunboat, and made me no reply; but I soon saw he had succeeded in forcing himself upon their notice at last, for he was flashing back question and answer rapidly now, as I judged by the frequent and hasty movements of his dancing mirror.

By and by he turned the ray upon my sofa again.

"Gunboat Hornet," he signalled in swift flashes, "Pacific squadron: party of twenty men sent ashore by admiral's orders to make arrangements for observing total eclipse of the moon on Saturday evening."

I was glad to hear it, for we began to feel the want of civilized society.

That same morning the doctor rode up to see me again, and brought me a very welcome present, a pair of crutches. On these I was now to be permitted to hobble about, and I took advantage of my liberty that very afternoon by stumping up, with Frank's aid, to the mouth of the crater.

While I stood there, supported on my two sticks, and watching the lava still grunting and grumbling as uneasily as ever, for it was clear that Pélé was in a grumpy mood and a big eruption was slowly brewing, we were joined by the officers and doctor of the Hornet on their eclipse observation expedition, accompanied by several sailors and natives, with ponies, tents, and other necessaries for camping out on the very summit, high above the level of the ordinary cloud-veil. The new-comers were surprised to find a scientific man already on the spot, in possession as it were, and gladly availed themselves of my knowledge of the mountain in choosing a good and suitable station for their tents and instruments.

I confess, after the terrors by which I had lately been surrounded, it was no small relief to me to find ourselves reinforced as it were by a strong and armed body of our own fellow-countrymen. I breathed a little more freely when I knew at least that help was at hand should we ever chance to stand in need of it.

I sent off Frank at once to show the naval men what seemed to me the best position on the whole mountain for pitching their tents and setting up their observatory, and, under my directions, he led them straight to a low peak on the right of Kalaua's, over-looking the crater and the Floor of the Hawaiians.

It was a jutting point with a good open platform on the very summit, composed of rock a good deal softer than the mass of basaltic lava which makes up in great part the cone of that vast and seething volcano. The men of the Hornet were delighted with my selection, which combined all the advantages of shelter and position, and began forthwith to unpack their belongings and settle themselves down in their new quarters. For myself. I hobbled back after a while to the house to rest and observe their actions through a field-glass from a distance.

Now, at any rate, we should be quite safe from any machinations of our Hawaiian entertainers.

As I reached the door Kalaua came out, his face all livid with anger and excitement. Evidently the new turn of affairs had greatly displeased him. He had been away all the morning, and had only just returned. His eyes were fixed now on the party on the summit, and some strange passion seemed to be agitating his soul as he watched their preparations for camping on the platform.

"Who are all these people here?" he cried out to me in English, flinging up his hand as soon as I was well within speaking distance, "and what do they want with their tents and their instruments here on the open top of Mauna Loa?"

"They're a party of English naval officers," I answered, "from a gunboat that has just steamed into the harbour, and they've come up by order of the admiral to observe the eclipse of the moon on Saturday."

Kalaua's countenance was an awful sight to look upon. Never before or since has it been my lot to behold a human face so horribly distorted with terror and indignation as his was that moment. His features were ghastly. They reminded me of the mask of his heathen ancestors. It seemed as if some cherished hope of his life was frustrated and disappointed, dashed to the ground at once by some wholly unexpected and untoward incident. "Kea," he cried aloud in Hawaiian to his niece within, "this is awful! This is unendurable! Come out and see! The English are camping on the Platform of Observation."

At the words, Kea sprang out upon the balcony from the room within where she had been sitting alone, and shaded her eyes with her hands as she looked up in an agony of suspense and expectation towards the distant peak. In a moment some sudden passion thrilled her. Then she clasped her fingers hard and tight in front of her, as it seemed to me with some internal spasm of joy and satisfaction. "I see them," she cried, "I see them! I see them."

"They shall never remain there!" Kalaua shouted again, stamping his foot on the ground with resolute determination. "If they stop there till Saturday, it will spoil all! I won't permit it! I can't permit it!" Then he turned to me more calmly, and went on in English, "I know a much better place than that, up on the left yonder, less exposed a great deal to the open wind and the glare of the volcano."

He pointed as he spoke to another peak, away off to the west; a peak that did not look down nearly so sheer into the hollow of the crater and the sea of fire. I had thought of that place too, and rejected it at once, as being in fact far more exposed and windy than the other.

I shook my head. "Oh, no," I said, "the peak they've chosen is by far the best one."

"You think so?"

"I am sure of it."

Kalaua turned away with an angry gesture. "Better or worse, they shall never camp there!" he exclaimed with warmth. "The Hawaiians are masters still in Hawaii. Whether they will or whether they won't, the Englishmen shall move their tents from that peak there. We will never allow them to occupy that spot. We will make them shift from the Platform of Observation."

"I don't think you'll find it easy to turn away an English detachment," I observed quietly.

Kalaua clenched his fist hard, and ground his teeth. "Anywhere but there," he muttered, "and there, never!"

He stalked away angrily with long hurried strides towards the point where Frank and the sailors, all unconscious, were pegging their tents and staking out their encampment with a merry hubbub. What happened next I could only observe vaguely at a distance through the medium of my glass; I learned the details afterwards more fully from Frank and the officers. But what I could notice for myself most clearly nearer home was this, that all the time while Kalaua was parleying with the Englishmen on the mountain, Kea stood still quite breathless on the verandah, watching the result of her uncle's action with the keenest interest and the wildest emotion. She watched so closely that I couldn't help feeling the result was a matter of life and death to her, and it somehow seemed to me that her hopes were now fixed entirely on the white men's resolve to maintain the position they had first taken up on the point of the mountain.

It was clear from what we saw that the Englishmen insisted on maintaining their position.

In about an hour, Kalaua returned, trembling with rage. "It's no use," he cried, "I can't turn them off. They will camp there. I've said my best, but I can't dislodge them: they must take their lives in their own hands." And he flung himself like a sulky child into an American rocking-chair on the broad verandah.

As for Kea, I saw her look up suddenly, with a wild flash of relief coming over her white face. Next moment, a fixed despair succeeded it. "No use, no use," she seemed to say to herself. "They will have to go yet. A respite, perhaps, but not a rescue."

Kalaua sat and rocked himself moodily up and down like one who resolves some desperate adventure.

When Frank returned late at night to Kalaua's, he told me the full story of that hasty interview. The old Hawaiian had gone up to the mountain determined to put a stop to the camp on the platform at all hazards. At first, his manner was all politeness and sweet reasonableness. He offered them water from the well at his own house, and he had come, he said, with the utmost suavity, to save them from choosing an unsuitable spot, and putting themselves in the end to immense inconvenience by having to move to some better position. He pointed out a thousand imaginary disadvantages in their present site, and a thousand equally imaginary points of superiority in the one he himself had selected for them. He knew the mountain from top to bottom: no one could choose as well as he could. But the officers stuck to their point steadily. This was the place to observe the eclipse from, and here they meant to camp out accordingly.

Wouldn't they at least sleep down at his house? No, thanks, they p>referred to camp out by themselves, according to orders, here on the open. Then Kalaua began to lose his temper. What right had they, he asked in a threatening voice, to come trespassing there on private property? The first lieutenant responded promptly by showing a letter from the King at Honolulu, authorizing the officers and men of the Hornet to choose a place for themselves anywhere on the open summit of Mauna Loa, all of which was Government demesne, with the solitary exception of Kalaua's garden. The old native's anger grew hotter and hotter. They couldn't say why, but it was quite clear that some private end of his own would be interfered with if the officers were allowed to camp out within view of the crater and the Floor of the Hawaiians. I had very little doubt myself, from what Frank told me, that some native superstition was at the bottom of his objection. I thought it probable there was a taboo upon the place, it was in all likelihood a seared spot of Pélé's.

I remembered the fate of the man who trod the Floor of Pélé and I wondered what would happen to our friends from the Hornet. However, in the end, as the naval men refused to be moved by either threats or entreaties, Kalaua retired at last in silent wrath, muttering to himself some unintelligible words about the folly of white men and the might of the volcano.

"Take care," he cried, as he turned on his heel, flinging back his last words at them. "You've chosen the most dangerous spot on the whole mountain. It reeks with fire. The rock about there is all inflammable. Mauna Loa will take care of itself. If you drop a match upon it, it'll burn like sulphur."

The officers laughed and took no more notice. They didn't know as well as I did how deep and fierce a hold heathendom still exercised over the minds and actions of these half-savage natives.

When Frank told me all this in the silence of our own rooms by ourselves that evening, my heart somehow sank ominously within me. "Frank," I said, "I don't know why, but I'm sure there's mischief brewing somewhere for us and for Kea. I wish we knew something more about this man Maloka they're always talking about. I feel that some terrible plan is on foot for that poor girl's marriage. The mystery darkens everywhere around us. Thank heaven, the English sailors have come to protect us."

"I asked several natives about Maloka to-day," Frank replied quietly; "but though they all knew the name, they only laughed, and refused to answer. They seemed to think it an excellent joke. One of them said he didn't trouble himself at all about people like Maloka. And then they all looked very serious, and glanced around as if they thought he might possibly hear them. But when I asked if Maloka lived near by, behind the peaks, they burst into roars of laughter again, and advised me not to be too inquisitive."

"Strange," I answered. "He seems to live close here upon the summit, and yet we never happen to come across him."

"Where's Kalaua now?" Frank asked.

"Gone out," I answered. "He went away early in the evening. Perhaps he's visiting his friend Maloka."

"I wish I could follow him," Frank cried eagerly. "I'd like to catch this Maloka by the throat, whoever he is, and I'll bet you sixpence, if I once caught him he'd be pretty well choked before I let him go again."

"Did the Hornet's men send down for water to Kalaua's well?" I asked.

"Oh, yes," Frank answered. "They took up some pailfuls."

"Humph!" I said. "I hope Kalaua hasn't put anything ugly into it."

CHAPTER XI

That night, like the nights before, I tossed and turned on my bed incessantly. The pain in my leg had come back once more. It was long before I dropped asleep by degrees. When I did sleep, I slept very heavily, almost as if someone had drugged or tampered with my drink at dinner.

In the stillness of the night, a sound again awoke me. I raised my head and gazed up suddenly. Could this be Kalaua and his friend again? No, not this time. A red glare poured in at the window. And it was Frank who stood with a warning finger uplifted close by my bedside in the glow of Mauna Loa.

"Tom," he whispered in a hoarse, low voice, "there's foul play going on, I'm certain. I see nobody in Kalaua's room, and just look how red it all is to eastward."

At the word, I jumped out of bed awkwardly, and crept to the window as well as my injured limb would permit me. Sure enough, a lurid light hung over the peak where the sailors were encamped: "Give me the glass!" I cried. Frank handed it to me hastily. I looked and saw a great glare of fire surrounding the tents with their white awnings. At first my eyes told me no more than that: after a while, as I grew more and more accustomed to the gloom, I could see that a dozen little points of fire were blazing away around the frail canvas shelters.

"There's something up on Mauna Loa," I cried. "An eruption!" Frank inquired with bated breath.

"No, no," I answered. "Not a mere eruption. Worse than that, a fire, an incendiary fire. The ground around them seems to be all one blaze."

"Kalaua said it was inflammable, you remember," Frank cried.

"But sulphur would never burn like that," I answered. "I fancy he must mean to turn them out by fair means or foul; and as far as I can see he's succeeding in his object."

"You think it's he who's set it on fire then?" Frank asked curiously.

"Run up and see," I answered. "The sailors are awake and moving about hastily; but perhaps you may yet be of some use to them."

"All right," Frank answered, "I'll be with them like wildfire."

In a minute he had tumbled into his coat and trousers, pulled on his boots, clapped his hat on his head, and run out lightly up the road to the encampment. By the time he reached the burning summit, I could see with the glass that the whole camp was in a perfect turmoil of wild confusion. The sailors were rapidly unpegging the tents and carrying away the instruments from the burning patch to a place of safety lower down the mountain. I could make out Frank joining eagerly in the task; he was helping them now with all his heart and soul. I only wished I too was there to second him. In this struggle of science against savage malignancy, my indignant sympathy went fiercely out on the side of knowledge. But my lame leg kept me painfully inactive.

Presently, in the dim light, far nearer home, I saw two men creep slowly down the crater path from the summit: two skulking men, with native scarves tied loosely round their waists; tall and erect, lithe and cautious. I recognized them at once; one was Kalaua, the other was his visitor of the preceding evening. They crept down with the air of men engaged on some criminal undertaking. In their hands they bore two empty tin kegs: I knew the shape well; they were American petroleum cans!

Like lightning the truth flashed through my startled brain. For some reason or other best known to themselves, these two secret votaries of an almost extinct faith desired to dislodge the eclipse-observing party from the peak that overhung and commanded the crater. They feared perhaps the wrath of their hideous goddess. Unable to move the Englishmen by force of reasoning, they had tried to drive them out from this sacred site by means of fire. They had saturated the porous and sulphurous soil here and there with petroleum. No pity, no remorse; they must have meant to burn them as they lay, for then, applying a match to it quietly, they had stolen away, leaving the flames to fight the battle in their absence against the sleeping white men, whom they had perhaps supplied with drugged water from the well in the garden.

At the gate they separated. It was a weird sight. Neither spoke, but both together bowed down thrice in the direction of the steaming crater. After that each placed his palms against his neighbour's. Then Kalaua stalked silently on towards his own house; his companion descended the zig-zag path that led right down to the Floor of the Strangers.

Could Maloka live in some cave of the platform? It was terrible to dwell in an atmosphere like this, an atmosphere of doubt, suspicion, and heathen treachery. Save for Kea's sake I would have left it at once. But Kea's fate bound me still to the spot. I must learn the truth about this terrible marriage.

For half an hour I sat and watched, while the observers on the hill-top ran to and fro in their eager desire to save their tents and baggage from the menaced destruction. Happily, they had waked before the fire reached them. At the end of that time, Frank and the first lieutenant came down with news. "How goes the fire?" I asked in breathless eagerness.

"Almost under now," the officer answered cheerily. "We've managed to put it out somehow for the present. But what can you do in the way of putting out fire when the very earth under your feet's inflammable! I never saw stuff burn like that. The flames spread at first on every side with just wonderful rapidity."

"Ah," I put in as carelessly as I could. "Lava, I suppose, and sulphur, and so forth?"

"H'm," the lieutenant answered with a dubious sniff. "You may call it sulphur and lava if you like; but for my part, I think it smelt precious like petroleum."

"You don't mean to say so!" I cried, astonished at this independent confirmation of my worst suspicions.

"Yes, I do," he answered. "That's just about the name of it. And petroleum doesn't grow of itself in Hawaii."

"Tom," my brother said, coming up to me quietly, and speaking in a very unwonted whisper; "this is not the place to discuss all these things. The sooner you and I can get out of it the better. It's my belief Kalaua has saturated the ground with something and set it on fire."

"I don't know what particular heathen did it," the officer put in with a confident tone; "but of this I'm sure, that somebody's poured coal oil all over the place. I smelt it distinctly. Now, I don't mind camping out on volcanoes or craters when they're left to themselves, but I'm hanged if I like them when they're stirred up with coal oil to go burning down the tent over a fellow's head. It's clear these Sandwich Islanders are inhospitable folk; they don't mean to let us pitch our tents on that particular spot; and if they can't turn us out one way, why then they'll turn us out in another. As it is, we've lost already two of our tents, and it was a blessing we didn't lose the whole lot together, not to mention the lives of Her Majesty's lieges to our care committed, for we were snoring most peacefully when the fire began."

"How did it all happen?" I asked with interest.

"Why, just like this. We were lying asleep, like warriors taking their rest, on our own mattresses, sound asleep, every man Jack of us, when I saw a glare shining under the tent, which I suppose would never have woke me if a spark hadn't happened to fall on my forehead. My first idea was that the volcano had got up an eruption on purpose in our honour: but when I got outside and looked at the ground, I came to the conclusion it couldn't be that for various reasons, and I set it down to your friend the native. For one thing, the place just reeked of petroleum, and for another, it was only alight on the surface, in half-a-dozen different places at once, exactly as if somebody had set a match to it."

"And what did you do then?" I inquired.

"Oh, I waked the men, and I never knew men so hard to waken. By dint of care however we've put it out, and I've come down here to talk the thing over with you."

"Well, what do you think you'll do now?" I asked.

"Why, the British tar doesn't like to be beaten," my new friend answered, "but I'm shot if I'm going to lie still and be roasted alive in my bed like a salamander. These fellows seem too shifty for us to deal with. Open fighting I don't object to, mind you, but I do object to baking a man to death unawares while he's sleeping. It's distinctly caddish. The other place seems a very decent one. It's not so good as this in some ways, I admit, but it'll do anyhow better than a baking. And as soon as we can get away down to Honolulu, we shall have the law against these petroleum-spilling brown fellows."

"You will get no redress," I said. "No Hawaiian will believe any story against Pélé. But at any rate you had better move for the present. Some evil will befall you if you stop where you are. Kalaua sticks neither at fire nor poison."

And sure enough, they were forced to shift their quarters next day to the place Kalaua had at first pointed out to them.

By this time indeed I will frankly confess, it was beginning to strike me that Kalaua's was not a safe place to live in. We had almost made up our minds indeed that as soon as the eclipse was well over, we would return on the Hornet to Honolulu. Kea's wedding alone could detain us longer: but my curiosity on that point was so strong and vivid that I determined to ask our new friends to wait till it was over, and then to take us with them to the neighbouring island. I couldn't bear to abandon her to Kalaua's mercy. Meanwhile, the sailors were busy with their own preparations, for the eclipse arrangements took up their whole time.

For the next few days accordingly Frank was all agog with this new excitement. He was running about all over the summit from morning till night, deeply engaged in the mysteries of tent-pegging, and absorbed in discussions of level, theodolite, telescope, and spectrum analysis. He was proud to display his knowledge of the volcano to his new friends. He showed the first lieutenant every path and gully round that terrific crater: leaped horrible fissures, yawning over abysses of liquid flame, with the junior midshipman; and made the good-humoured and easy-going sailors teach him marvellous knots, or instruct him in the art and science of splicing. As for me, I hobbled about lamely on my crutches as well as I could, envying him the ease with which he did it all, and longing for the time when I too might get about up and down the crater on my own two legs, without let or hindrance.

"Sailors are awfully jolly fellows," Frank confided to me one evening, after a day spent in exploring and setting up instruments. "Upon my word, do you know, Tom, if I wasn't so awfully gone on volcanoes, I think I'd really run away to sea and be a gallant midshipmite."

"For my part I don't care for such dangerous occupations," I answered prudently, gazing down with pensive regret into the slumbering crater, that heaved now and then uncomfortably in its sleep with the most enticing motion. "A storm at sea's an unpleasant sort of thing. I don't like all that tossing and plunging. Give me the peace and quiet of dry land, with no more excitement than one gets afforded one by an occasional eruption or a stray earth-quake, just to diversify the monotony of every-day existence."

And indeed I could never understand myself why anybody should want any more adventurous life than that of a sober scientific man, with a taste for volcanoes. None of your hurricanes and tornadoes for me. A good eruption's fun enough for anybody.

The point finally selected by the naval men for their camp and observatory lay at some considerable distance from Kalaua's house, but full in view from the open verandah. It was difficult of access however in spite of its position, because a huge gully or rent in the mountain-side, descending to several hundred feet below, intervened to separate us; and the interval could therefore only be covered by something like half an hour's hard riding. I was not able myself accordingly to assist at any of their preparations; I could only sit on the verandah like an idle man, and watch them through a good field-glass, which enabled me to follow all their movements intelligibly, and to interest myself to some small extent in the details and difficulties of their extensive arrangements.

During these few remaining days, before the expected eclipse, Kea sat with me often on the verandah doing nothing, for her work on her trousseau was now all finished; but she seemed more pre-occupied and self-centred than usual, as if dreading and hating her expected marriage. I felt sure she disliked the husband they had chosen for her. Often when I spoke to her she brought her eyes back suddenly, as if from a great distance, and sighed before she answered me, like one whose mind has been fully engaged upon some very different and unpleasant subject. She asked me much too, at times, about her father's brother and friends in England, about the life in our quiet home country, about people and places she had heard her father talk about in her early childhood. She knew them all well by name; her father, she said, had loved to speak of them to her. Evidently he had been one of those wild younger sons of a good family, who had left home early and gone to sea, and taking to a roving Pacific life had fallen in love with some young Hawaiian girl, Kalaua's sister and Kea's mother, for whose sake at last he had made his home for life upon a lofty peak of these remote islands. His family, displeased at his marriage, no doubt, had all but cast him off; and even if they invited Kea to come home to them in England after his early death, they would have had no great affection, one may easily believe, for their little unknown half-caste kinswoman. Yet I felt sure if only they could once have really seen Kea they must have loved her dearly, for there was something so sweetly pathetic and winsome in her child-like manner that no one who saw her could help, in spite of himself, sympathizing with her and liking her.

"Are there any volcanoes in England?" Kea asked me once, after a long pause, with sudden energy.

"Unhappily, no," I answered, with a quiet sigh of professional regret. "That's my one solitary cause of complaint against my native country. It's disgustingly free from volcanic disturbances. Britain is much too solid indeed for my private taste. It affords no scope for an enterprising seismologist. There were some good craters once, to be sure, in geological times, at Mull and Cader Idris, but they're all extinct long since. We haven't a volcano, good, bad, or indifferent, anywhere nearer us than Hecla or Vesuvius."

"Then I should love England," Kea replied very quietly. "Oh, Mr. Hesselgrave, if that's so, what on earth made you ever leave England to come to such a country as Hawaii?"

She spoke so earnestly, that I hardly liked to tell her in cold blood, I came just for the sake of those very volcanoes which seemed to impress her own private fancy so very unfavourably. There's no accounting for tastes. I've known people who loved yachting and didn't mind a bear hunt, yet wouldn't go near an eruption for a thousand pounds, and could hardly even be induced by the most glowing descriptions to look over the edge of a sheer precipice into the smoking crater of an active volcano. Some folk's prejudices are really astonishing! As if volcanoes weren't at bottom the merest safety-valves to the internal fires of our earth's centre!

The few remaining days before the date of the eclipse passed by, I am happy to say, uneventfully. I was grateful for that. Excitements indeed had come so thick and fast during these late weeks that a little quiet was a welcome novelty. And the presence of our English friends from the gunboat gave us further a sense of confidence and security to which we had far too long been strangers. We knew now, at least, that a British war-vessel lay moored in the harbour below to watch over our safety.

On one of the intervening evenings, as I sat in the verandah smoking a cigarette alone in the pleasant cool of tropical twilight, I heard two natives, hangers-on of Kalaua's, talking together in the garden, where they were busy picking fruit and flowers for the use of the house on the grand occasion. At first I paid little heed to their conversation: but presently I thought I overheard among their talk the mysterious name of that strange Maloka. I pricked up my ears at the sound. How very curious! Then they too were busy with the great event. I listened eagerly for the rest of their colloquy.

"What are the flowers for?" the younger man asked, as he laid some roses and a great bunch of plumbago into a palm-leaf basket.

"Garlands and wreaths for Maloka's wedding," the elder answered in a hushed and lowered voice.

"It will be a very grand affair, no doubt," the younger went on quietly. "They've made great preparations. I saw the dress that Kea is to wear, and the bridesmaids' veils. Very fine, all of them. Quite a festival! Shall you go and see it?"

"If Kalaua allows me," the other answered.

"She's a pretty young girl," the younger man continued in an unconcerned voice, still filling his basket. "A great deal too good to my mind for a wretched creature like Maloka. What does an ugly fellow such as that want with a young and beautiful wife like Kea? I'd give him some ugly old crone to match himself, I can tell you, if only I had my way about it."

"Hush," the elder answered with a certain solemn tone of awe in his voice I had often noticed the natives used when they talked together about this unknown bridegroom. "Maloka may be ugly and dark if you will, but he is a grand husband for any girl to light upon. You young men nowadays have no respect for family or greatness. It is a proud thing for a girl to marry such a bridegroom as Maloka."

"Well, as far as I'm concerned," the young native answered, with a slight toss of his head, "I don't think so much as you do of the whole lot of them. The family's all very well in its way, but an ugly girl would be quite good enough for a fellow of that sort. What's the use of throwing away beauty like hers upon Maloka? Nicely he'll treat her. However, it's no affair of mine, of course; her uncle and herself have settled the wedding. All I shall do is to go and look on. It'll be worth seeing. They say it's going to be the grandest wedding that ever was made in all Hawaii since King Kamehameha's daughter was married long ago to another member of the same family."

The old man laughed at this, as if it were a joke: but somehow his laughter sounded painfully grim. I felt that whatever Maloka's family might happen to be, and it was clear that the natives thought it a very distinguished one, it was not famous for kind treatment of the unhappy women it took as brides to its illustrious bosom. My heart was sore for poor little Kea. To be sure, she acquiesced in the marriage, no doubt, but then girls will sometimes acquiesce in anything. It was painful to think she was going to marry a native whom even coarse, common natives like these regarded as unworthy of her on any ground except that of family connection. But the Hawaiians, I knew, have still to the full all the old barbaric love of aristocratic descent and distinguished ancestry. "A good match" would atone for anything.

At last the Saturday of the expected eclipse arrived in due time, and all the day was occupied by Frank and the naval officers in final arrangements for their scientific observations. At Kalaua's house, too, great preparations seemed to be going on; it was clear some important event was at hand: we almost suspected that Kea's wedding must be fixed for the Sunday, or at least the Monday morning following. Kea tried on all her things early in the day, I believe; and many Hawaiian girls came in to help her and to admire the effect of the veil and trimmings. But a less merry wedding-party I never heard in my life before. A cloud seemed to hang over the entire proceeding. Instead of laughing and talking, as the natives generally do on the slightest provocation, we could hear them whispering below their breath in solemn tones in Kea's room, and though lots of flowers had been picked and arranged for the occasion in long wreaths and garlands, the girls didn't make sport, as usual, out of their self-imposed task, but went through with it all with profound and most unwonted sombreness of look and movement. Kea had said her betrothed was somebody of very great importance. I began to think he must be someone so awfully important that nobody dare even smile when they thought or spoke of him! I had never heard of any one quite so important as that before, except the head master of a public school; and it seemed in the highest degree improbable that Kea should be going to marry the Provost of Eton, or the Principal of Clifton or Cheltenham College.

When evening drew on, we all had supper together at Kalaua's, the naval officers, Frank, and myself, and then the eclipse observation committee went off under Frank's efficient guidance round the long gully to their chosen station. I meant to observe them there through my field-glass myself, and see what sort of scientific success was likely to attend their arduous labours.

For a while I sat and mused in silence. The house seemed unusually still and lonely after Frank left. Kalaua, Kea, and the native servants were none of them loitering about on the verandah or in the sitting-room, where they generally lounged. I seemed to be in sole possession of the establishment, and I hobbled out by myself a little way on to the platform in front of the house, wondering what on earth could have become of all the inhabitants in a body together. My leg was nearly well now, I could get along nicely with the aid of the crutches. I was almost sorry indeed I hadn't tried to ride a horse, game leg and all, and go round with the eclipse party to the camp of observation.

Yet somehow I felt uneasy, too, at Kea's absence, and my uneasiness was increased, I don't know why, by the constant glare that overhung the crater. The lava was unusually red-hot to-night; the great eruption we had long expected must surely be coming. I hoped it would wait till my leg was quite well; a lame foot is more than enough to spoil the whole pleasure of the best and finest volcanic outburst to an enthusiastic amateur. I went back to the house and called twice for Kea. Nobody answered. My suspicions were quickened. I ventured to open the door of her bedroom. It was empty—empty! All the wedding-dresses and wreaths and veils were gone from their places, where I had often observed them when the door stood ajar in the course of the morning. A vague sense of terror fell upon my soul. What could all this mean? Where was Kea? and why was she out at this time of night, with all her friends, and in her wedding garments?

I called a third time, and nobody answered. But out on the platform in front of the house I saw an aged Hawaiian hag, a witch-like old woman who hung about the place and lighted the fires, sitting crouched on the ground with her arms round her knees, and grinning hideously at my obvious discomfiture.

"Where's Kea, old lady?" I cried to her in Hawaiian, as well as I could manage it.

The horrible old woman grinned still more odiously and maliciously in reply. "Gone out," she answered, mumbling her words in her toothless mouth so that I could hardly make them out or understand them.

"Where to?" I asked angrily, for I was ill at ease.

"How should I know?" the old woman growled back. "I suppose to the festival."

"The festival! Where? What? When? Whose festival?"

"The festival of Maloka," the old hag mumbled with a cunning smile.

With a sudden horror I remembered then that Maloka was the mysterious person to whom, as I concluded, Kea was engaged, the person whom she and Kalaua had so often mentioned in their low and whispered talk with one another.

"Who's Maloka?" I cried, sternly laying my hand upon her withered shoulder, "Quick! tell me at once, or it will be the worse for you."

"He's Pélé's son," the old hag answered, chuckling to herself with a horrible chuckle. "He lives with his mother, his angry mother, away, away, down in the depths of Mauna Loa. He's Pélé's favourite. She loves him dearly: and she often asks for a wife for Maloka."

In an instant the whole hideous, incredible truth flashed wildly across my bewildered brain. They were going to sacrifice Kea to this hateful god! They were going to fling her into the mouth of the crater! They were going to offer her up in marriage to the son of Pélé!

CHAPTER XII

"Which way have they gone, you hag?" I cried, shaking her in my fierce anger.

The old woman raised one skinny brown finger, and pointed with a grin in the direction of a zig-zag path which lay to the left of Kalaua's roadway.

Without waiting one second to deliberate, or question her, I set off at once upon my crutches, bounding and scurrying over the ground like a kangaroo by successive leaps, and hastening forward at a brisk rate which I should have thought beforehand no crutches on earth would possibly have compassed.

I reached the path, and turned hastily down it. The track was rough and difficult to traverse, even for an active man with both his legs to go upon; but for me, in my present halt and maimed condition, it was terribly hard and all but impracticable. Nevertheless, impelled by horror and fear for poor Kea's safety, T hurried along at a mad rate down the steep zig-zag, careless whether I fell or not in my wild haste, but eager only to prevent I knew not what awful heathenish catastrophe. I only prayed I might yet be in time to save her life. After many stumbles and hairbreadth escapes, rolling over and over with my crutches by my side, I found myself at last on the Floor of the Strangers, not far from the spot from which I had fallen before, but separated from it by a narrow chasm in the black basalt, a chasm, riven deep in the solid rock, and filled below, as I saw at once, with a fiery strait of white-hot lava.

It was full moonlight. Away off to the left, on the summit of the mountains, I saw the camp-fires of the naval eclipse parties. They were standing there, etched out distinctly against the pale sky-line;

and I could recognize every one of their faces with ease through that clear air in the bright light of a tropical moon. But not a sign of Kea was to be seen anywhere. I looked anxiously round for her, and met no token anywhere. The old woman must surely have misdirected me on purpose. Fool that I was to have believed that hag! Kea and her party could hot have come this way at all towards the crater.

I saw my mistake. They had sent me wrong by deliberate design! At this supreme moment Kalaua had intentionally attempted to escape my notice.

Suddenly, as I looked and wondered in awe, a strange procession began slowly to descend the mountain side opposite, beyond the chasm, into the mouth of the crater. At its head came the man in the feather mask whom I had seen that day that I broke my leg on the edge of the precipice, and whom I now more distinctly than ever recognized as indeed Kalaua. There was no mistaking his gait and carriage. He stalked on proudly in front of the procession. Next after him, bearing rods with bunches of feathers fluttering in the breeze from their tops, came the four acolytes who had stood by his side that awful morning when he solemnly devoted me to the devouring volcano. Then four Hawaiian girls in white bridesmaids' dresses, with long garlands of oleanders strung round their necks, followed in order, two by two, waving their hands slowly above their heads, and chanting native himenés, as they call their long monotonous wails and dirges. My heart stood still as I saw with horror that Kea walked last, with downcast eyes, habited in her full bridal dress, and with the white veil falling round her in folds almost to her ankles. Behind her straggled a few hushed and awe-smitten spectators, half friendly assistants at this ghastly ceremony. I saw them all clearly but two hundred yards off, though the chasm in the rock with its red mass of molten lava below separated me from them far more effectually than a mile of intervening distance could possibly have done.

My first impulse was to cry aloud with indignation and horror. My next, for Kea's sake, was to hide myself at once behind a black jagged pinnacle of hardened lava before they caught sight of me. I did so almost as soon as the procession began to file slowly past the turn of the road; and it was by peering with caution round the corner of the pinnacle that I had observed them all as they descended two by two along the narrow foot-path.

Step after step they moved gradually down, to the long-drawn music of those unearthly himenés. Kea, in particular, glided on like a ghost, with downcast eyes and shrinking demeanour, yet not so much in the manner of a victim as of one who willingly and heroically devotes herself to some terrible end for the good of her country.

I knew she believed she was averting the wrath of Pélé, and I gasped with horror at her awful resolution.

Presently, the procession reached the Floor of the Strangers, on whose platform I myself was already crouched flat, though always separated from me by that terrific chasm; and advancing still to the lugubrious sound of these doleful himenés. Kalaua placed himself on the edge of the precipice, at the very spot where I myself had fallen over in pursuit of the butterfly. Kea, moving forward with slow and solemn steps, stood at his right hand, in her bridal dress, with her bloodless fingers clasped downward in front of her.

Then Kalaua began, in a strange cramped voice, to drone out some horrible dedicatory service. It sounded like the service he had droned out over myself on the morning of my accident: but I understood Hawaiian much better now, and could follow the words of his frightful litany with very little difficulty. Crouching behind the shadow of my broken lava pinnacle, I saw and heard the whole savage orgy like some unseen presence in that vast and self-lighted natural cathedral.

"Great Mother Pélé," Kalaua began, intoning his words on a single note and dividing his address into curious irregular verses—"Great Mother Pélé, who dwellest in the fire-lake, Queen of the Hawaiians, we, thy children, bow ourselves down in worship before thee.

"We assemble in thy temple, oh, thou, that delightest in the flesh of white-skinned chickens: we come into the outer threshold of thy house, oh, thou, that ridest on the red flaming surges.

"Sugar-cane, and tappa-cloth we offer to thy children: a bride, a wife, to thy favourite, to Maloka.

"Five sons thou hast borne in thy home, below; and one is humpbacked; thy favourite Maloka.

"A white man came from the lands beyond the sea: a pale-faced stranger; a wanderer to Hawaii.

"Of thy own accord thou chosest him a victim for thyself. He fell into thy trap. The white man's foot trod forbidden ground: the Floor of thy children, of thy children, the Hawaiians.

"In thy wrath, thou rosest to crumple him to ashes: thy flames soared upward like tongues of fire; dancing and surf-riding on the billows of flame, didst thou put forth thy red right hand to seize him.

"Come forward, Kea!"

The trembling girl came forward timidly.

Kalaua continued his awful chant once more, shaking his robe, and slowly dancing.

"A maiden rescued him: a mortal maiden. She stole the victim from the clutches of Pélé.

"No hand might save him against thy will: the force of a mortal avails not against the fiery might of a living goddess.

"Thou, Pélé, lettest him go for very contempt; thou gavest up the prey from thy fingers willingly.

"For such as her, a law is laid down.

"Victim for victim: life for life: whoever snatches an offering from Pélé, himself must satisfy the wrath of the goddess.

"Were it not so, thou wouldst deluge the land with lava; thou wouldst swallow the towns in the jaws of earthquakes: thou wouldst lick up the cane-fields with red tongues of fire.

"Thy son, Maloka, thy favourite, the humpbacked, he cried aloud to his mother for the maiden in marriage.

"'Give me this girl, he cried aloud, Oh Pélé: give me this maiden who snatched away thy victim.'

"Thou, Pélé, madest answer: 'My son, I give her thee.' Thou didst turn uneasily in thy flaming home, and threaten the Hawaiians with a deadly vengeance.

"See, we bring her: and we give her to Maloka; willingly, of her own accord, the maiden comes: on Maloka's night, arrayed as a bride in snow-white raiment, eager for her fate.

"Come forward, attendants!"

The bridesmaids, in their wreaths and garlands, stepped forward. I listened, horror-struck.

"Kea, do you take this god, Maloka, for your wedded lord?"

In a stifled voice, tremulous but firm, Kea answered aloud in her soft Hawaiian, "Kalaua, I take him."

"Maloka, do you take this girl, Kea, for your wedded wife?" And even as he spoke Kalaua cast something invisible from his hand with a dexterous throw, into the yawning abyss of lava below him. I then observed, for the very first time, that while the ceremony went on, the lake of fire had risen by slow degrees in the crater, and stood flush now with the Floor of the Hawaiians.

The volcano, as if in response to his direct question, gave a hideous roar, excited, I suppose, into some minor eruptive effort by the object he cast into it, which seemed to crash down and break upon a smouldering smoke-stack. It was as though the mountain had answered back in words, "Oh, priest, I take her."

Kalaua leaned forward, shaking and agitating his sacrificial robes. "At the stroke of midnight," he went on solemnly, "at the actual moment when Maloka the humpbacked climbs aloft to put out the moon, we will take the bride into the bridegroom's chamber. When Maloka the humpbacked puts out the moon, then leap, Kea, into the arms of your husband. See, see, how lovingly he stretches out his fiery arms for you in his chamber below there! When he rises in his might to put out the lamp that rides in heaven, then leap into his embrace. 'Tis the signal he gives you! Till then, sit still, and await your husband!"

Kea sat down by the edge of the precipice, on an isolated block of black basalt, and leaning her little chin on her small white hand, gazed below in awe and silent expectation on the flood of lava.

I knew, then, exactly what Kalaua meant. At the precise moment of the total eclipse, Kea was to leap into the abyss of the volcano.

I took out my watch, and consulted it anxiously, It wanted more than half-an-hour still to the actual point of absolute totality. I had that half-hour only to save Kea in. I saw her there seated on the edge of the abyss. I knew that the moment the moon was finally obscured, she would rise from her place, and leap madly forward of her own accord, into that sea of lava. She thought it her duty to appease the goddess. How to rescue her I could form no plan. Even if I rushed forth in my horror and managed by some miracle to span with a leap that yawning chasm that spread so wide between us, what was one lame white man among so many wild and heathenish Hawaiians? I could do nothing. I was helpless, powerless. If I set out to call the naval officers to my aid, long before I reached them, Kea's charred and mangled corpse would be floating, a mass of blackened ashes, on the fiery flood in the still rising crater. I trembled with horror. And yet—and yet—

And yet I must do something to rescue Kea!

CHAPTER XIII

On the summit above, all unconscious of this ghastly and incredible tragedy taking place within a stone's throw of where they stood, I could see Frank and the men from the gunboat, busying themselves quietly with their eclipse arrangements, as if nothing more terrible than an ordinary volcanic outburst were proceeding anywhere in their immediate neighbourhood. The bright tropical moonlight revealed their forms and faces to me almost as clearly as the noonday sun: I could even distinguish the play of their features, and notice how Frank was laughing and talking, with his usual good-humoured boyish merriment, to the officers and sailors. The contrast was nothing short of appalling. On one side, those easy-going sea-faring men, with their finished instruments of modern science, calmly engaged in observing and noting down the face of our distant satellite: on the other side, that group of stern and sombre half-heathen Hawaiians, occupied in the horrible and cruel rites of an effete and proscribed barbaric religion. Never, I thought to myself, did civilization and savagery stand closer together, cheek by jowl: never did the two extremes of human thought and human sentiment come in nearer contact, all unconscious and heedless one of the other. For neither party could see round the corner of jagged rock that overhung and divided them; I alone, looking either way up and down the crater, could take in both groups at a single glance, the scientific observers and the wild heathen priests of that human sacrifice.

But how to attract the notice of the Englishmen! If only I could manage to catch Frank's face! If only I could fling up my arms and sign to him to come! But he would not look! It was terrible! It was agonizing!

Suddenly, an inspiration seized me unawares. The heliograph to the rescue! I might signal to him by the moonlight. One chance yet left! My mirror! My mirror!

I felt for it in my pocket with trembling fingers. One moment of hope. Then an abyss of despair. I had left it at home by the sofa at Kalaua's. That chance was fruitless.

To have made my way back for it would have been of little avail. I could not fail in that case to attract Kalaua's keen attention, as I hobbled painfully in the broad moonlight up the zig-zag path: and to attract attention under existing circumstances would probably mean all the sooner to hasten poor trembling Kea's impending fate. I must think of some other means of communicating with Frank. I must find some less obtrusive and dangerous way of calling the sailors and officers to our assistance.

How short a time still remained to us! I took out my watch and gazed at it hopelessly.

In another burst of inspiration, then, I saw my way clear. A mirror! A mirror! all ready to hand! I could signal still! I could call their attention!

My watch was a gold one, a naval chronometer: the inside of the case was burnished and bright. I held it up straight in the bright beams of the moon, and as Frank's face turned for a moment in the direction where I stood, or rather crouched under cover of the pinnacle, I flashed the light full in his eyes from the reflecting surface. Thank heaven! Thank heaven! he started and observed it. I signalled three rapid flashes for attention. Frank flashed me back, yes, from his own pocket mirror. My hands shook so that I could hardly hold the watch aright: but with tremulous fingers I managed somehow to spell out the words, "Come quick. Bring sailors. Steal cautiously round the dark corner. There's foul play on. Kalaua means to make Kea leap into the crater as a bride to Pélé's son at the moment of totality."

In a second, I saw that Frank and the officers had taken it all in in its full ghastliness, and that, if time enough remained, Kea might yet be saved from that awful death in the fiery abysses. Without one moment's delay their men seized the horses, and leaving one or two, officers alone to continue the observations, dashed wildly down the ravine, and into the gloom of the gully.

Then, for a few minutes more, I lost sight of them entirely.

When they emerged again to view, on the Floor of the Strangers, they had left their horses, and, headed by Frank in his white jacket, were creeping cautiously, unperceived, under cover of the broken masses of lava, round the sharp corner of the jutting platform. My heart bounded as I saw them approach. There was still some chance, then, of saving Kea!

Had she been my own sister I could not have felt the suspense more awful.

As we gazed below we saw, to our dismay, that the lake of fire was still tossing and rolling with wild wreathing billows, and that it had risen visibly several feet in the last few minutes.

While we still looked, the moon's face began slowly to darken. The eclipse had commenced. We had only a quarter of an hour yet to the period of totality.

In a few short words, I explained to Frank and the sailors he had brought with him the entire situation in all its gravity. I told them all I had seen and heard; and their own eyes confirmed my report: for there stood Kea full in view, round the corner of the pinnacle, beyond the open chasm, in her white dress, with her hands clasped in inarticulate prayer, and her pale face turned up appealingly towards the cold moonlight. She had but a quarter of an hour left to live. Yet near as we were to her, it would have taken us more than fifty minutes to ride round the crater by the outer rim to the only practicable path on the other side of the chasm.

"What are we to do?" I cried, in my horror, though in a low voice, for it was necessary above all things not to arouse the Hawaiians' quick attention.

"We must cross the chasm somehow," the eldest officer of the party answered at once. "We can't let the poor girl be sacrificed before our very eyes."

"If we only had a rope, and could once get it fastened on the other side, we might sling ourselves across, hand over hand," Frank suggested eagerly.

"We have rope, lots of it, on my saddle over yonder," the officer answered. "But we can't get it fastened. If only the chasm were narrow enough to leap! But it's quite impossible. No athlete on earth could ever jump it."

"Stop!" Frank cried. "The bamboo! The bamboo!—I had a big bamboo down here the other day, stirring up lava in a liquid pool in the small craters. There it is—over yonder. I think with that—"

He said no more, but creeping over for the bamboo, crawled noiselessly on with it to the edge of the chasm. We all followed him on our hands and knees, skulking behind the pinnacles, and concealed from the Hawaiians by the rough lava-masses. I seemed to forget my half-mended leg in the excitement of the moment, and to crawl along as easily and as quickly as any of them. On the very edge of the deep fissure, now boiling below with liquid fire, Frank laid across the bamboo from cliff to cliff, so that it hung, a frail bridge, across that yawning abyss of sulphurous vapour. With great difficulty, he thrust it home on the far side into a honey-combed mass of crumbling scoriae lava.

"Now stand, you fellows, on the end," he said, "to give it weight and keep me from slipping. I'm the lightest of the lot: it'll bear me, I suppose, if it'll bear anybody. I'm going to cross it, hand over hand, and take a rope with me for you others to come over by. If it breaks, I shall fall into the lava below. No matter: it's jolly white hot down there now; it'd frizzle me up, if it came to the worst, before I could feel it."

The sailors brought all their weight to bear upon the loose end. I knelt by myself, breathless with suspense, to see the result of this mad experiment. The bamboo was frail and supple indeed: if it broke, as Frank said, all would be up with him. But Frank was too brave to heed much for that. He tied the rope round his waist in a running noose, caught hold of the bamboo with both his hands, and swinging himself off the edge with a quiet and gentle swaying motion, so as to lessen as far as possible the strain of that slender bridge, hung one moment like a gymnast, from a trapeze, suspended between the sky and the gulf of liquid lava.

It was a terrible moment. All eager with excitement, we leaned over the abyss, and watched him rapidly but quietly passing hand over hand across that frightful chasm. As he reached the middle, the bamboo for one indivisible second of time bent ominously down under his light weight. Would it yield? Would it crack? If so, the next instant we should see him falling, a lost life, into that hideous strait of liquid fire. For half a throb of the heart, our agony of doubt and suspense was unspeakable. Next instant, he had passed in safety the central point; the weight was easier; the faithful bamboo curved slowly up again.

We breathed more freely. He had reached the far end; he was grasping the cliff, the further cliff, in eager confidence, with that brave young hand of his. The lava was loose; all bubbly with holes like a piece of rotten pumice-stone. "Frank, Frank," I cried in a low voice, but beside myself with terror, "take care how you trust it. The stuff's all dry. It never can bear you. Don't try to grasp it!"

"All right," Frank answered low, as he struggled on. "There's no foothold anywhere near the edge. I must go in for a somersault. Thank goodness that gymnasium work I used to hate so has done something for me unexpectedly at last."

As he spoke, he vaulted with a light leap on his hands up the edge of the precipice. The next thing we knew, he was standing, safe and sound, with the rope round his waist, a living soul, on the further brink beyond the chasm.

A sigh of relief burst simultaneously from all our lips. "Now, quick!" the officer cried. "Not a moment to be lost! Swing yourselves over, men, and make haste about it!"

Frank held the end of rope in both hands firmly, twisting it for greater security twice round his body: and the slenderest of the sailors, trusting himself the first to this safer bridge, crossed over the chasm with the ease and rapidity due to long practice on the masts and rigging. As soon as he had landed unhurt on the far side, he helped Frank to hold the end of the rope; and one by one his five companions and the officer last of all made good their passage in the self-same manner. I alone was left to keep up touch and facilitate their return to the hither side; for we felt we must probably fight for Kea. Our plan was to seize her by main force, before the natives were aware, retire with her to our horses, and ride down at all speed to the Hornet at Hilo.

"Now, look sharp: make a dash for it!" the officer said, in a muffled voice. "Out into the open, and seize the girl at once! Never mind the men. Carry her off in your arms before they know what's happening, and back here again to the rope immediately."

I stood and watched on the further bank of that fiery strait. The moon's light meanwhile had been growing each instant dimmer and dimmer. The greater part of the orb was already obscured. The moment of totality was rapidly approaching. Kea, warned by a word from her uncle, stood up in her bridal dress and faced the awful flood of surging lava. Kalaua, by her side, began once more to drone out in long notes his monotonous chant. He flung a handful of taro, with a solemn incantation, into the mouth of the volcano. "See, Pélé," he cried, "we bring thee thy daughter-in-law. See, Maloka, we bring thee thy chosen bride. At the stroke of midnight, at the appointed hour, thou hast put out the lamp in heaven, the moon. This is thy signal: we mortals obey it. O humpbacked favourite of Pélé the long-haired, the bride will go into the bridegroom's chamber. Maloka, hold up thy hands for thy handmaid! leap, Kea, leap, into the arms of your husband!"

I looked and trembled. Kea stepped forward with marvellous courage. Through the dim light of the ruddy volcanic fires I could see her draw back her white veil from her face, and make as though she would meet some lovers embraces. Then the last corner of the moon disappeared all at once in darkness from my sight, and for half a moment, at that critical point, I saw and heard nothing with distinctness or certainty.

Next instant, as if by magic, a weird red glare illumined the scene. Great arms of fire lunged forth spasmodically from the open crater. Maloka had leaped forward with his scorching hands, to claim his bride in fiery wedlock. The eruption had at last begun in real earnest. Huge volumes of flame darted up with commingled black smoke towards the vault of heaven. A lurid light hung upon the massive clouds overhead. Stones and ashes and cinders fell wildly around us. The crater had broken loose in its fiercest might. The rivers of liquid fire were welling up all round and bursting their bounds with majestic grandeur.

And in the midst of all, by the uncertain light of that deep red glare, I could just see Frank and the friendly sailors bearing off Kea in her bridal robe, half fainting, half unwilling, before the very eyes of the astonished and amazed Hawaiians. Our party had rushed upon them from behind, unawares, at the very first instant of total eclipse, and seized her in their arms, in the act to jump, from the circling ring of baffled natives.

Thank heaven, then, they had been in time; in time to save her from the cruel volcano and the crueller superstition of her heathen ancestors.

"Back, now, back, to the chasm and your horses!" the officer cried in a tune of command, at the top of his voice, as Kalaua and the natives, recovering after a moment from their first shock of surprise, and gathering together into an angry knot, began to show signs of attempting an organized resistance. "Carry off the girl between you, there, at the top of your speed. No time to lose! The lava's rising." He pointed his revolver. "And if one of you heathen brown fellows come a single step nearer," he added with a menace, "I'll put a bullet through his ugly black head, as soon as look at him."

Kalaua leaped forward with a wild and almost inarticulate cry of rage and disappointment. "Seize them, friends," he shrieked aloud in his hoarse Hawaiian. "Kill them! Tear them to pieces! How dare they interfere with the bridals of Maloka?" Bat even as he spoke, a river of lava burst suddenly forth from the mouth of the seething crater, and spread a broad stream of liquid fire between the infuriated natives and the little band of Kea's gallant protectors.

"Run, run," Kalaua cried. "Down the other road! By the black rocks! Intercept them at the gulley. Kill them! kill them! They're Pélé's enemies! However you do it, kill them, kill them!"

The officer, unheeding their savage threats, stalked on to the chasm, and pointed firmly but quietly to the rope that still spanned it. Kea, dazed and frightened, yet graceful and light of limb as ever, clasping it hard in her small fair hands, swung herself across to my side with native ease, while the sailors held the ends of the cable on the bank opposite. Then one by one the others followed swiftly in turn, with admirable discipline, in spite of the shower of ashes, till only Frank was left by himself beyond the deep abyss of boiling lava.

"How will he ever get over?" I cried, looking across at him in alarm and terror.

"Oh, don't be afraid, old fellow!" Frank shouted back cheerily. "Leave that to me! I'm as right as ninepence. Thank goodness, I can hang from a rope like a monkey!" And with a hasty movement, he began to roll the end of the cable tight around his waist and to tie it firmly in a slip-knot to his sturdy shoulders.

How he could ever drop himself down so steep an abyss with flame below, I had no notion. On the other hand, I knew he dared not trust the bamboo again. It had bent already too severely with his weight, almost indeed to the point of breaking; and half charred as it now was with the constant heat ascending for ever from that subterranean furnace, it would no doubt have snapped short in the middle by this time, if he had been foolish enough to attempt crossing by its aid a second time over the few yards of chasm that intervened to divide us.

Frank however had a device of his own. Planting his feet hard against the edge of the precipice, he swung himself off like a monkey, with the rope grasped hard in his two hands; and even as he fell, kicking off from the side, he gripped it quickly hand over hand, till he brought himself up with wonderful agility level with the opposite side where we were all standing. Half a dozen stout arms were extended at once to pull him safe to solid land; and in another moment we all stood secure, with Kea in our midst, a recovered party, on the brink of the crater, undeterred by anything more serious in its way than an ordinary everyday volcanic outburst.

"Off to the horses!" the officer cried aloud; and before I knew what was happening, two of the sailors had seized me in their arms, and were hurrying me away at a break-neck pace up the steep zig-zag to the level of the summit.

In the ravine, we came, sure enough, upon the horses, tethered and guarded by a couple of sailors. "Mount," the officer cried with military promptitude: and the men mounted, not exactly, I must confess, with the ease or grace of cavalry orderlies. I mounted myself, too, with what skill I could command, taking into consideration that broken leg of mine; and giving the trusty little ponies their heads, we rode at full speed in breathless haste, but in long Indian file down the narrow bridle path to the base of the mountain.

I knew well the gully where the two roads joined, and where Kalaua had threatened to meet us in hostile array with his proscribed band of heathen followers. It was an ugly spot, with great overhanging rocks to defend the pass, and if they got there first, I knew we should have to fight them for possession of Kea. All depended now upon the swiftness and sureness of foot of our ponies. To be sure, we were mounted, while Kalaua and his party were all on foot; but then, most of us had been greatly delayed by the necessity for recrossing the chasm on the rope bridge in order to get at our path and our horses; and even apart from this unavoidable stoppage, very few ponies, at the best of times, can cover the ground faster than an unimpeded Hawaiian. Those fellows can run like a deer or greyhound. I trembled for the result if they held the rocks above the fort in full force. They could hurl down stones upon us from the heights with infinite ease, crush us like locusts as we passed beneath them: even fire-arms there would be useless against a party that held the pass in any numbers.

On, on, we rode, in fear and trembling. The volcano now was all in full blast. Ashes and pumice stone kept falling around us. Smoke and steam obscured our way. But the dangers of nature frightened us little in comparison; what we dreaded most was the desperate onslaught of the enraged Hawaiians.

As we drew near the fort however I breathed again more freely. Not a sign of Kalaua was anywhere to be seen. We rode along, cautiously, under the overhanging rocks. No Hawaiian showed his grim black head above or below us. Then Kea, with a shriek, guessed in a moment exactly what had happened. "The lava has overwhelmed them!" she cried, clasping her hands together in girlish trepidation. "They are dead! They are dead! My uncle! My people! Pélé will not be robbed of her victim at any rate. The lava has burst forth in one great flood and swallowed them."

And indeed, when we reached a turn in the bridle path, and looked up the ravine down whose rugged centre the other road descended tortuously, a terrible sight met our astonished eyes. The summit of the mountain was now one red and lurid mass of living fire. Through the gully along whose course Kalaua and his followers had plunged in the first darkness of the total eclipse to cut off our retreat, a vast river of red-hot lava was pouring onward resistlessly in huge fiery cataracts. We could see the fierce stream descending apace over ledges of rock like a flood of molten metal poured forth from the smelting-bowl; we could see it engulfing trees and shrubs and stumps and boulders in its plastic mass; we could see it overwhelming the whole green ravine with one desolating inundation of fire and ashes. "Quick, quick," I cried; "ride, ride for your lives. You may think volcanoes are nothing much to be frightened of; but, I tell you, a volcano in such a temper as that is not by any means a thing to be trifled with. She's mad with rage. The stream's coming down the valley straight for the fork; take at once to the ridge, and ride on for your lives. Ride, ride across country, anyhow, to the Hornet at Hilo!"

"And me!" Kea cried, looking back at me appealingly, for she headed our little hasty procession. "What's to become of me? Of me, who have brought it all by my sin upon you! Of me, for whose sake Pélé is so angry! Of me, who roused her wrath by stealing away her victim! Leave me here to die! Kalaua is dead! My people are swallowed! I meant myself to die in their place, but you wouldn't let me! Leave me here to perish! If you don't leave me, Pélé in her anger will pursue you on your way to the sea itself, to the foot of the mountain!"

"Ride on!" I answered. "Ride on to Hilo. Is this a time to make plans for the future? We'll discuss all that, Kea, on the deck of the Hornet."

That evening, on board the British gunboat, lighted up by the terrific glare overhead, we had time to reflect what it all meant, and to feel ourselves free to think and speak again.

"What will you do now, Kea?" I asked the poor girl, as she sat there, trembling, in a small cabin chair, while the red flames still illumined for miles and miles the summit and flanks of Mauna Loa. "Do you wish to stop here in your own island?"

Kea looked up at me with a half terrified glance. "I wish," she said in a low voice, "to be as far away from Pélé and Maloka as possible..... Kalaua is dead. Pélé has devoured him..... I will leave my husband on my wedding night. I will go home to my father's people."

"That is best so," I answered quietly. "Hawaii is no place for such as you. I don't think Maloka will ever miss you. We will go on the Hornet away to Honolulu. There you can take passage with Frank and me on the next steamer for San Francisco, on your way home to dear, peaceful England."

"Why," Frank exclaimed, with a look of immense surprise, "you don't mean to say, Tom, you're going to turn your back upon a volcano—and in actual eruption, too, into the bargain!"

"Bother volcanoes!" I answered testily. "One may have too much of a good thing. I don't care if I never set eyes on another eruption as long as I live. So that's flat for you."

"Nonsense!" Frank promptly replied with spirit, refusing to desert an old friend in a moment of vexation. "That's all very well now, when you're annoyed with Pélé for misbehaving herself; but I'll bet you sixpence, in spite of that, you'll be off again before twelve months are over, exploring some other jolly crater in Sumatra or Teneriffe, or the Antarctic regions."

And sure enough, as I put the last finishing touches to these lines for press, the post brings me in a letter in an official envelope, "On Her Majesty's Service," informing me that the Lords Commissioners of the Admiralty have been graciously pleased to accept my suggested appointment for three years on a scientific mission to investigate the volcanic phenomena of Cotopaxi and other craters in the chain of the Andes. By the same post, I have also received a note from my sister, who is now stopping down at the Kentish rectory where Kea lives with her English relations, and who says, among sundry other pieces of domestic criticism, "What a dainty, charming, lovable girl your pretty little Hawaiian really is, Tom! So gentle and good-natured, and so sweetly pensive! I can hardly believe, myself, there's anything of the cannibal Sandwich Islander in her! She's as fair as I am, and quite as European in all her ideas and thoughts and sentiments. When she doesn't talk nonsense about Pélé, in fact, I almost forget she isn't one of ourselves, she's so perfectly English. But the rector says he can't allow her to teach in the Sunday school till she's quite got over that heathenish rubbish. By the way, I shouldn't be surprised if she and her Cousin Hugh were some day to make a nice little match of it, if only Hugh can ever persuade her that it wouldn't be bigamy, and that she isn't already duly married to some ugly, mythical, humpbacked creature of the name of Maloka."

www.ingramcontent.com/pod-product-compliance
Lightning Source LLC
Chambersburg PA
CBHW061458170626
46811CB00004B/1569